a novel

Walking
ON ICE

a novel

Walking ON ICE

Maria Pilatowicz

TATE PUBLISHING
AND ENTERPRISES, LLC

Published by Tate Publishing & Enterprises, LLC
127 E. Trade Center Terrace | Mustang, Oklahoma 73064 USA
1.888.361.9473 | www.tatepublishing.com

Tate Publishing is committed to excellence in the publishing industry. The company reflects the philosophy established by the founders, based on Psalm 68:11,
"The Lord gave the word and great was the company of those who published it."

Book design copyright © 2011 by Tate Publishing, LLC. All rights reserved.
Cover design by Erin DeMoss
Interior design by Chelsea Womble

Published in the United States of America

ISBN: 978-1-61346-929-3
1. Fiction / Historical
2. Fiction / Coming of Age
11.12.27

Dedication

For Edward

Acknowledgments

Included in this story are random clippings from daily
newspapers *Express Wieczorny* and *Zycie Warszawy*, covering years 1953-1954.

Wieczysta chwała Stalinowi

Dziś w stolicy Kraju Rad

WIELKI WÓDZ I NAUCZYCIEL CAŁEJ POSTĘPOWEJ LUDZKOŚCI

spoczął obok Włodzimierza Lenina w Mauzoleum na Placu Czerwonym

Dziś o godzinie 12 czasu moskiewskiego trumna z ciałem Józefa Stalina spoczęła w Mauzoleum na Placu Czerwonym w Moskwie.

W godzinach rannych w Sali Kolumnowej w Domu Związków przy trumnie Józefa Stalina zebrali się członkowie Komitetu Centralnego Komunistycznej Partii Związku Radzieckiego, członkowie Rządu Radzieckiego, członkowie Komisji dla Zorganizowania Pogrzebu, marszałkowie, generałowie.

Niewypowiedzianie ciężkie są ostatnie chwile pożegnania. Kierownicy Partii i Rządu zdejmują trumnę z ciałem Józefa Stalina i powoli kierują się ku wyjściu z Sali Kolumnowej. Za trumną niesione są wieńce oraz na aksamitnych poduszkach ordery i medale. Trumna złożona została na lawecie armatniej. Przy dźwiękach marsza Beethovena rusza kondukt pogrzebowy. Józef Stalin udaje się w swą ostatnią drogę na Plac Czerwony.

Plac Czerwony wypełniony jest po brzegi morzem ludzi. Są tu przedstawiciele rzesz pracujących Moskwy oraz delegacje republik związkowych i autonomicznych, krajów i obwodów całego ogromnego państwa radzieckiego. Na trybunie korpus dyplomatyczny. W absolutnej ciszy zastygły szeregi oddziałów wojsk garnizonu moskiewskiego.

W głębokim, pełnym bólu milczeniu wita Plac Czerwony kondukt pogrzebowy. Kondukt zbliża się do Mauzoleum. Trumna z ciałem Józefa Stalina zostaje ustawiona na podwyższeniu. Kierownicy Partii i Rządu powoli wchodzą na trybunę Mauzoleum. Rozpoczyna się zgromadzenie żałobne.

W głębokim skupieniu wysłuchają zgromadzeni przemówienia Przewodniczącego Rady Ministrów ZSRR i Sekretarza KC KPZR G. M. Malenkowa, który daje wyraz ogromnemu bólowi narodów radzieckich po stracie Wielkiego Wodza Józefa Stalina i wyraża zdecydowaną wolę narodów radzieckich doprowadzenia do zwycięskiego końca dzieła Józefa Stalina — budowy komunizma. Ogromną mocą tchną słowa Malenkowa: „Nie ma takiej siły na świecie, która by była w stanie przeszkodzić narodowi radzieckiemu w jego zwycięskim marszu do komunizmu. Naprzód do triumfu wielkiego dzieła Lenina-Stalina".

Następnie żegnają Józefa Stalina pierwsi zastępcy Przewodniczącego Rady Ministrów ZSRR — Beria i Mołotow.

Po zakończeniu wiecu żałobnego kierownicy Partii i Rządu schodzą z trybuny, podnoszą trumnę i kierują się z nią do Mauzoleum. Płyną dźwięki marsza żałobnego Chopina. Godzina 12. Rozlegają się werble i salwy artyleryjskie. Orkiestra gra hymn państwowy Związku Radzieckiego.

Trumna z ciałem Józefa Stalina spoczęła w Mauzoleum obok sarkofagu Włodzimierza Lenina. Kierownicy Partii i Rządu wchodzą z powrotem na trybunę. Obok nich zajmują miejsca marszałkowie i generałowie Armii Radzieckiej. Orkiestra gra marsza wojskowego. Jednostki garnizonu moskiewskiego defilują przed Mauzoleum, gdzie spoczywają Lenin i Stalin, oddają ostatni hołd pamięci Wielkiego Wodza narodu radzieckiego. Wodza wszystkich prostych ludzi na całym świecie — Józefa Stalina.

Uchwała
Rady Państwa i Rady Ministrów
o uczczeniu pamięci Józefa Stalina

Dla uczczenia [...] cych i Jej [...] Ministrów [...]

1. Zgo[...] nej [...] Nar[...] wick. Katow[...]

STALINOGRÓD

a województwo katowickie na województwo

STALINOGRODZKIE

2. Pałacowi Kultury i Nauki, stanowiącemu dar Związku Radzieckiego dla stolicy Polskiej Rzeczypospolitej Ludowej, ofiarowany z ini-

Stalin zawsze z nami

We wszystkich miastach i miasteczkach polskich, we wszystkich polskich wsiach, zalegia dziś uroczy-

To Jemu i kierowanej przez Niego partii zawdzięczamy, że polskie dziecko uczy się dziś w polskiej

---

This was the time I often asked, "Why?" and as often was told I was too young to understand. Now I'm also too old to remember. What appears to me as truth is bound to be full of gaps. As I'm trying to remember, my mind tends to fill these gaps, to create an orderly and comprehensible reality. It pieces together small, factual, but random elements into larger, logical constructions. And, although these constructions are logical, they are also fictitious. By filling these gaps, I'm trying to make sense of our lives—Sophie's, Janie's, Theo's, mine. I need to know if anyone can be saved from oneself. If and how our lives could have been different.

How to Remember Sophie?

It was frightfully cold. The way it usually was in these parts in January or February. The continental, eastern wind seemed to find every small opening in the already worn winter coat Sophie had on. She fought against the wind and clouds of whipped-up snow, which was hard and icy, and pelted her face like flying pearly kasha before it's cooked. It was late afternoon, and the lights were coming on in some windows. She missed her friend Agnes. Agnes was so much stronger. If only she were here, they would hold hands and the wind wouldn't be so bad.

When she reached the entry to her building, she felt exhausted. In the stairwell she leaned her backpack against the railing and rested, looking up into the circular well of steps winding and winding above her. She had to go all the way up to the fourth floor, so she was in no hurry. She started slowly, and soon the rhythmic sound of her snow boots over the steps put her into a semi-trance. She was still rocking back and forth to the same rhythm when she rang the doorbell. She waited a while listening for the footsteps, but there was no answer. She pushed the bell again and leaned lightly against the door. It gave under pressure and opened wide. She stepped inside, wondering why it was unlocked.

There must have been a window open in one of the rooms because suddenly there was a powerful draft, which slammed the entry door behind her. She stood in the dark and realized that the closest door was to her father's study, directly to the right. She took a step, reached out, and found the doorknob. It felt very cold and smooth. She turned it and pushed the door open. In the soft gray light flowing from the window, her father's body was darkly outlined, hanging from the light fixture in the ceiling. She did not see his face. He was turned away, toward the light. Everything in the room was wrapped in the various shades of grayness from charcoal to pearl. The only thing that claimed any color, any life to itself, was the crimson cord used to hold up draperies in the study. Now it cut through the grayness leading from the back of his neck to the ceiling.

Sophie's backpack became extremely heavy, so that she had to sit down on the floor, right there in the doorway. For an indeterminable length of time, she sat there watching her father's body sway and turn slightly as the sheer curtain hanging loose in the window moved back and forth, obedient to the gusts of wind.

Yes, I remember Sophie very well. I remember myself. I remember us. We were very close then. We huddled under one umbrella when it rained and staggered together, holding hands, when the snow was knee deep on the sidewalks. In class we sat next to each other, and I remember sometimes quickly glancing at her profile and thinking how beautiful she was and how I loved her.

In the late spring, when afternoons were already long and warm, we sat straddling the garden wall, facing each other. We tirelessly swung our legs and talked a flowing river. Without conclusions. Without destinations. It felt as good, as if we were connected to the flow of life itself. The connection between us felt good; it filled us with energy and excitement.

Her father was arrested at the end of June 1952, and our entire small street knew about it. The next day she missed school, and immediately after I wanted to run and see her.

"Agnes, you come here this minute and sit your wiggling behind on that kitchen stool!" my mama said. "Keep your busybody nose out of other people's trouble. I want you to stay away from Sophie—at least for a couple of days."

"But why, Mama, why? She is my best friend!"

"You are much too young to understand any of this. You'll just have to take my word for it. It's not safe. *They* are probably watching the building."

"Who are *they?*" I asked.

"You don't need to know that just yet. Now run along and play in the yard."

I climbed the garden wall and sat there by myself. I thought about Sophie and about her father who was a gentle and funny man. I wondered who *they* were and in what way her father was a criminal. I wondered if Sophie knew what he'd done and if she was hurting the same way I was hurting for her. I sat there all afternoon and swung my legs very fast.

After he was arrested, she refused to talk or to think about him. Any time she did or saw something trivial that brought his face into her mind; she would deliberately turn away from it, and from him. He was being punished; he was being forgotten, Sophie thought, for deserting her. July was very hot, and their flat, which was on the top floor, was like an oven at the end of the day. She was trying to get away from the heat that came in waves from the buildings and pavements as well. She walked away from the small streets and clusters of apartment buildings, which indicated the proximity of the city limit. She remembered Tessa, her older sister, telling her there used to be fields of cucumbers and corn out this way. There was also a small house, now empty and boarded up, where the farmer who owned the fields used to live. Tessa told her about the baby goat he had kept behind the fence and that she had fed it yellowish blades of grass and old streetcar tickets she found in her pockets. Now some of the fields were leveled, others already dug up for the foundations of the long apartment buildings that the government co-op was putting up there. Almost against her will, the slightly hunched, slim silhouette of her father took shape in her mind. They used to walk here together sometimes at dusk or when the evening was very warm. They were walking here just a few days before he…

The stars had already been out, and she remembered looking up at them suspended out there, half way up in the great dark vault of heavens. It felt as if she was in an old Gothic church, its slim, straight arches curving beyond the stars

"Look," her father said, "there is Orion."

"Where, where?" Her eyes eagerly scanned the heavens.

"There, it looks like a kite. God's kite," he said, laughing.

They had this game going between them that required each to build upon and add to the imagination of the other. Sophie was almost eleven and knew God did not fly kites, but she fell right into the imaginary game, which her father initiated.

"Does it have a string?" she asked.

"Yes, it does," he said, "and it reaches half way around the world."

"And does God hold it in his own hands?"

"Well, of course He does. He loves to fly kites," her father said, putting his arm around Sophie's shoulders.

After a minute or so of silence, Sophie looked up at him and said, "Then He is not here. I mean, He is elsewhere. Not watching over me or you, just flying His kite."

For a moment her father's face became serious, and he looked into the darkened fields. Then in a voice barely audible he mumbled what she thought was, "Possibly, quite possibly." She didn't know what he meant but felt it wasn't a part of the game anymore, and she was suddenly afraid.

No one spoke about his arrest. But I could feel their glances sliding off my back like snakes when Sophie and I silently walked the school hallways during break. We never spoke about it either. When I saw Sophie after a week's absence, she was pale, and said she had trouble falling asleep. She neither cried nor mentioned her father. She just held my hand very tightly.

In my mind I kept turning over the questions of who and why, but, overwhelmed with everyone's silence, I was afraid to hear my own voice. I lurked about the rooms and hallways of my own home, trying to catch the scraps of hushed conversations, which would fade to whispers at the sight of me.

The weather also turned oppressive. It was the beginning of July, and the air was hot and heavy. The swallows were making tense little shrieks flying low, catching flies just a few feet above the ground.

There was the dream that periodically came back to her in the night, and Sophie would twist and moan in her bed until she would wake up in a sweat, whimpering like a small dog. She'd be climbing stairs, which led to their flat, for a very long time. Looking back into the stairwell, she could not see where they had begun. All she had left behind were vague shapes and shadows wrapped in a blue gray mist. She felt tired, and her book bag was getting heavier and heavier. The straps were cutting painfully into the flesh on her shoulders. Finally, she would reach the door. She knew it was hers because it was yellow, and yellow meant caution.

She would carefully open it and enter the darkened hallway. The study was to the right, and she knew she had to go there first. She'd reach for the doorknob, but she could not bring herself to open the door. Her hand would melt into the metal. Her fingers, polished like brass, glowed in the darkness of the hall. She could neither open the door nor detach her hand from the doorknob. She'd want to scream, call for help, but no sound would come from her open mouth.

After Sophie's father was arrested, I became aware of tensions, undercurrents, shadows, whispers, nods, half words, syllables, communicating things I did not understand. I became aware of my mother religiously closing shutters, drawing drapes at dusk, no matter the weather, and of my father watching the street from the darkened room. I persistently listened to the lowered voices through half-opened doors. Something Sophie's father wrote was printed in a foreign newspaper. French, I think. Behind the word *they* lurked a larger, indefinable, abstract, but ominous, presence. He was arrested because of what he wrote, I concluded. And then I wondered what one could put in ink on a page that would be so dangerous, so infinitely evil.

Sophie's father was unexpectedly released at the end of October. Sophie and I were looking through old magazines at the dresses women used to wear when her mother called us into the kitchen to eat some soup. Tessa, Sophie's older sister, also came from the other room. It was then that her father just walked in. Right before we finished the soup.

Sophie got up from her chair, stepped back, and watched while her mother and Tessa screamed and climbed all over him. He was still holding them both in his arms when he looked at Sophie. She was gray and motionless, lifeless like a stone.

I felt out of place in there, with them. I sneaked out and ran, as fast as I could, to tell my mother what had happened. She first asked how he was, how he looked, and I suddenly realized that he looked very thin and had a beard. Then I remembered his left hand resting on Tessa's dark hair. It was corpselike, yellow, and limp. I told my mama about his thinness and his beard, but I couldn't bring myself to mention the hand. I felt ashamed for having seen it at all, as if I had caught a glimpse of a very private part of him.

While he was gone, she was good, very good, at pushing him out to the margins of her mind where his presence lingered, wrapped up in the gray mist like the stairwell from her dream. The day her father came back, when they looked at each other, Sophie knew it wasn't going to be, for them, the same as it was before. Both of them were no longer the same as before. There would be no more walks in the fields, no more games. She did not welcome his presence. She sensed something altered, something disturbing about him.

She woke up one night in early December and heard the murmur of a hushed conversation coming from the next room. She got out of bed and stood cold and motionless for awhile next to the door of her parents' room. It was ajar, and she could hear the whispers and see two red points glowing in the dark. Each of them, she imagined, was a glowing core, an intense, red, pulsating center of a being. But then she smelled the smoke. Again they were smoking cigarettes and talking. Smoking and talking about things she was not supposed to hear. She recognized her mother's agitated whisper. "Don't say that, Aleks. You shouldn't even think that. We have two children…" Her whisper trailed off, and Sophie heard quiet, muffled sobbing. She shivered, turned around, and went back to bed. Lying awake with her eyes wide open, she thought about Orion—God's kite—and its string winding half way around the world.

When I say "I remember," how do I? Where do I start? An object, an image, or just a phrase, a single word? Are these the frayed beginnings of the thread to be picked up, untangled and unwound?

The thread is uneven. Thick at some places and at others thin, almost invisible. You stumble upon knots so tight you wonder if perhaps they are better off left untied than loosened, shedding fibers you'd rather not finger. "I remember" is risky. At times it's even lethal. The word *they* is a beginning of a thread… December 1952…

Mama was dicing dried apricots and raisins for the Christmas *placek.*

"Aggie, pull up the kitchen stool and sit next to me," she said, and I knew this was serious. The kitchen stool had always been an indicator. She had something important to tell me.

"This is about Sophie," she said. "I know her father is back, but that does not necessarily mean anything. He can be taken away again at any time. So far he's been called back twice, and he's come back every time. But one day he might not be so lucky."

I was growing restless on that stool, and I wished she would come to the point. Instead she suddenly asked, "Have you seen that brown car that's been parked every day down the street by the grocery? Well, *they* are in it. *They* are watching the building, watching Sophie's father."

"But he rarely even comes out of the house anymore," I protested. "Sophie says it's strange because he just sits there, locked up in his study. Sometimes he doesn't even speak a word to anyone all day."

"Yes," Mama said, "it is strange, and that's good enough reason for you to spend more afternoons at home instead of playing at Sophie's."

"But, Mama, she is my best friend and the only person that lives close enough," I tried to argue.

"The less traffic there is between our two households the better. If *they* are watching, *they* will be suspicious," Mama said, lowering her voice.

This time I was determined to find out who *they* were. I was, after all, almost twelve. I felt sure that almost twelve was old enough to know.

"Who are these people you keep calling *they*, and why are *they* so mad at Sophie's father?"

Mama looked up at me, fidgeting on the edge of the kitchen stool.

"You are still very young," she said, "but I'll tell you this: *they* are State Security men; *they* have power over all of us in the same way *they* have power over Sophie's father. What's happening to him can happen to anyone."

What she said was outrageous. It was inconceivable that adults like my father and Mama, and Sophie's parents, and other grownups like Uncle Henry or my teacher Mrs. Pawlak would be frightened of the men sitting, day in and day out, in the brown car at the end of the street.

"How come I never see any of these men hurting anyone?" I said.

"It's for the same reason many other important things, dear, which decide about how we are and how we live are obscured, hidden under the surface. In our lives there are more things that are concealed than those in plain view. And those in plain view are not always what they appear to be."

"I don't understand," I protested, but she already got up to rinse off her sticky fingers.

The sound of her voice came interspersed with the sloshing of water falling to the bottom of the metal sink. "Just remember what I said, and you will someday. In the meantime, do not talk about it to anyone you don't know or, for that matter, not to anyone you do. The next few days, you'll be helping me with Christmas cooking and cleaning, so no more visits to Sophie."

Express Wieczorny

Nr 37 Rok VIII   Warszawa. Piątek, 6 marca 1953 r.   Wyd. A   Cena 20 gr

Przestało bić serce Józefa Stalina

5-go marca o godz. 9 min. 50 wieczorem

zakończył życie Wódz i Nauczyciel postępowej ludzkości

Od Komitetu Centralnego
Polskiej Zjednoczonej Partii Robotniczej
Rady Ministrów i Rady Państwa
Polskiej Rzeczypospolitej Ludowej

DO ROBOTNIKÓW, CHŁOPÓW I INTELIGENCJI
PRACUJĄCEJ!
DO KOBIET POLSKICH I MŁODZIEŻY!
DO ŻOŁNIERZY POLSKICH!
DO NARODU POLSKIEGO!

Towarzysze i Obywatele!

Całe postępowe ludzkość z najwyższym bólem przyjęła tragiczną wieść o zgonie największego Człowieka naszych czasów — Józefa Stalina. Wraz z narodami Związku Radzieckiego szczególnie głęboko i boleśnie przeżywa ten wielki cios naród polski, który Towarzyszowi Józefowi Stalinowi zawdzięcza swe wyzwolenie z ponurej hitlerowskiej niewoli, swe odrodzenie, odzyskanie prastarych Ziem Polskich, utrwalenie swej niepodległości.

Masy pracujące Polski wiedzą, że ich historyczne przeobrażenia społeczne, wyzwolenie z jarzma obszarników i kapitalistów, zdobycie władzy przez lud pracujący i emancipacja państwa ludowego, olbrzymie osiągnięcia w budowie nowego życia — wiążą się nierozerwalnie z braterską pomocą narodów radzieckich, z serdeczną troską i ojcowską opieką Wodza i genialnego Nauczyciela mas pracujących całego świata, Wielkiego Przyjaciela naszego narodu — Józefa Stalina.

Od Komitetu Centralnego Komunistycznej Partii ... ZSRR
...ch członków Partii, do wszystkich ludzi
pracy Związku Radzieckiego

DRODZY TOWARZYSZE I PRZYJACIELE!

Komitet Centralny Komunistycznej Partii Związku Radzieckiego, Rada Ministrów Związku Socjalistycznych Republik Radzieckich i Prezydium Rady Najwyższej ZSRR z uczuciem głębokiego bólu powiadamiają Partię i wszystkich ludzi pracy Związku Radzieckiego, że 5 marca o godzinie dziewiątej minut pięćdziesiąt wieczorem, po ciężkiej chorobie zakończył życie Przewodniczący Rady Ministrów Związku Socjalistycznych Republik Radzieckich i Sekretarz Komitetu Centralnego Komunistycznej Partii Związku Radzieckiego, Józef Wissarionowicz Stalin.

Przestało bić serce współbojownika i genialnego kontynuatora dzieła Lenina, mądrego Wodza i Nauczyciela Partii Komunistycznej i narodu radzieckiego — Józefa Wissarionowicza Stalina.

Imię Stalina jest bezgranicznie drogie naszej partii, narodowi radzieckiemu, masom pracującym na całym świecie. Wraz z Leninem towarzysz Stalin stworzył potężną partię komunistów, wychował ją i zahartował; wraz z Leninem towarzysz Stalin był źródłem natchnienia i Wodzem Wielkiej Socjalistycznej Rewolucji Październikowej, założycielem pierwszego na świecie państwa socjalistycznego. Kontynuując nieśmiertelne dzieło Lenina, towarzysz Stalin poprowadził naród radziecki do historycznego w skali światowej zwycięstwa socjalizmu w naszym kraju. Towarzysz Stalin poprowadził nasz kraj do zwycięstwa nad faszyzmem w drugiej wojnie światowej, co w sposób zasadniczy zmieniło całą sytuację międzynarodową. Towarzysz Stalin uzbroił partię i cały naród w wielki i jasny program budowy komunizmu w ZSRR.

Śmierć towarzysza Stalina, który oddał całe swe życie ofiarnej służbie dla wielkiej sprawy komunizmu, jest najcięższą stratą dla partii, dla mas pracujących Kraju Rad i całego świata.

Wieść o zgonie towarzysza Stalina wzbudzi głęboki ból w sercach robotników, kołchoźników, inteligencji i wszystkich ludzi pracy naszej Ojczyzny, w sercach żołnierzy naszej mężnej Armii i Marynarki Wojennej, w sercach milionów ludzi pracy we wszystkich krajach świata. W tych dniach pełnych bólu wszystkie bratnie narody naszego kraju jeszcze bardziej zespalają się w wielkiej zwartej rodzinie pod wypróbowanym kierownictwem partii komunistycznej, stworzonej i wychowanej przez Lenina i Stalina.

Naród radziecki żywi bezgraniczne zaufanie i przepojony jest gorącą miłością do swej ukochanej partii komunistycznej, bo wie, że służenie interesom narodu jest najwyższym prawem całej działalności partii.

Robotnicy, kołchoźnicy, inteligencja radziecka, wszyscy ludzie pracy naszego kraju nieugięcie realizują politykę, opracowaną przez naszą partię, odpowiadającą żywotnym interesom mas pracujących, zmierzającą do dalszego wzrostu potęgi naszej socjalistycznej Ojczyzny. Słuszność tej polityki partii komunistycznej potwierdzona została przez dziesięciolecia walki, doprowadziła ona masy pracujące Kraju Rad do historycznych zwycięstw socjalizmu. Natchnione tą polityką narody Związku Radzieckiego pod kierownictwem partii niezachwianie kroczą naprzód ku nowym sukcesom budownictwa komunistycznego w naszym kraju. Masy pracujące naszego kraju wiedzą, że dalsza poprawa dobrobytu materialnego wszystkich warstw ludności — robotników, kołchoźników, inteligencji, maksymalne zaspokojenie stale rosnących potrzeb materialnych i kulturalnych całego społeczeństwa zawsze było i jest przedmiotem szczególnej troski Partii Komunistycznej i Rządu Radzieckiego.

Naród radziecki wie, że wzrasta i krzepnie zdolność obronna i potęga państwa radzieckiego, że partia ze wszech miar umacnia Armię Radziecką, Marynarkę Wojenną i organa wywiadu, aby stale wzmagać naszą gotowość do odcięcia druzgocącej odprawy każdemu agresorowi.

Polityka zagraniczna Partii Komunistycznej i Rządu Związku Radzieckiego była i jest niewzruszenie polityką utrzymania i utrwalenia pokoju, polityką walki przeciwko przygotowywaniu i rozpętywaniu nowej wojny.

The morning of March sixth was gray and cold. The wind tugged at the black, leafless branches of the trees outside the kitchen window. Sophie wedged herself into her customary spot between the table and

the windowsill. She was half done with her oatmeal when they said on the radio that Comrade Iosif Vissarionovich Stalin was dead. She stopped eating and listened to the broadcast. She turned the word dead over on her tongue a couple of times without making a sound. It filled her with both a familiar icy dread and morbid fascination. There was only one instance in her short life when Sophie came close enough to death to feel it. It involved her red cat Eric and her green parakeet Bugle. She held Bugle for a long time on the open palm of her hand. His corpse was unexpectedly heavy for a bird and very, very still. The tension and the small, inner trembling she felt whenever she had held Bugle when he was alive were gone now. She wondered if some giant had cupped his hands around Comrade Stalin when he was alive, or around her father, would he also feel the same tension and trembling she felt while holding Bugle? Was this tension and trembling the only difference between being dead and alive? Was this all there was to it? The question why her father chose death over life was never far from her mind. Sophie struggled to translate what she experienced holding Bugle while he was still alive into more human terms, and the word fear came to mind.

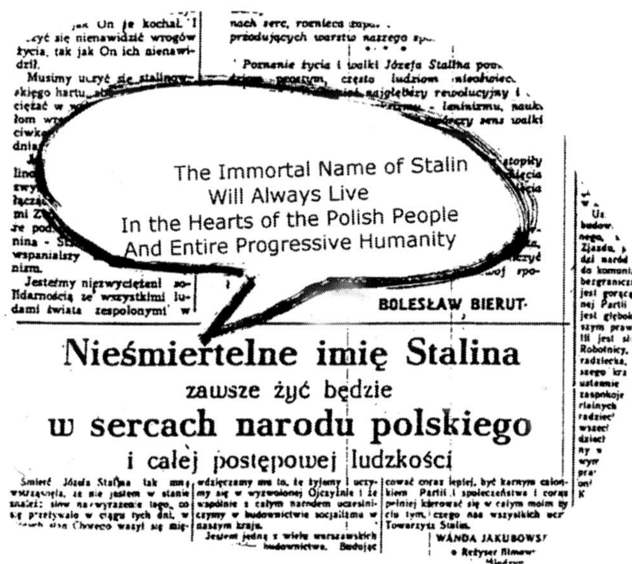

Parents are always trying to protect us from our own life, and it is always futile. My parents went to Sophie's father's funeral, leaving me behind with Aunt Rita, who came to keep me company. Later, Mama told me Sophie was not there either. She was sent away for awhile to stay with her mother's sister, out in the country. Mama never mentioned Sophie's father, but that was not necessary. I learned every grisly detail from the other kids on the street. The affair was morbid enough to be discussed repeatedly and at length during play. But I continued to think about Sophie. Where was she? What was going on in her head now? How, in what terms did she think of the dead? How did she feel, knowing death as close as she did? Would she remain the same, or would she be different after that?

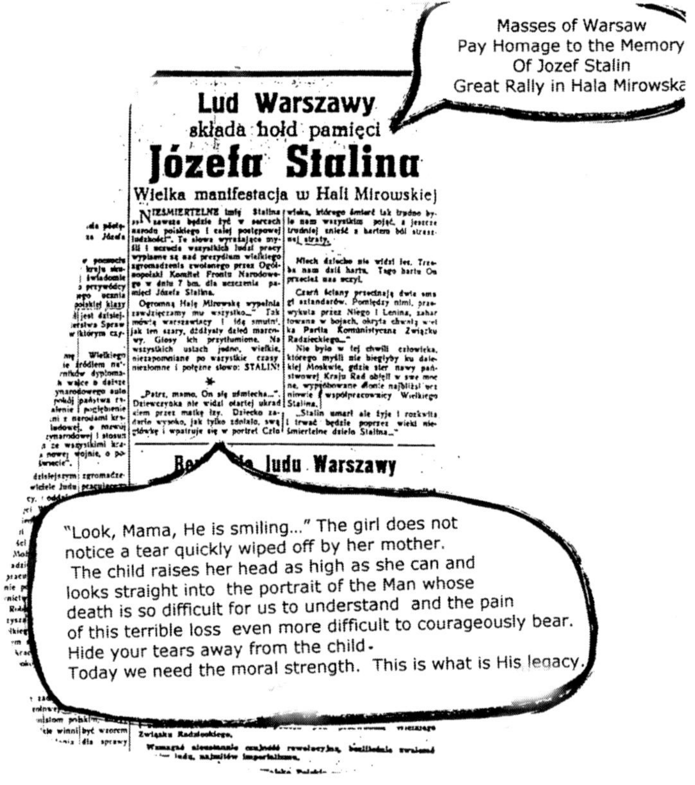

Sophie came back to school on the day Comrade Vissarionovich Stalin died. I was surprised to see her standing at the end of our class, lined up by twos along the wall in the gym. I was late, and there was no time to talk to her then. I watched her from my place in the line and thought she reminded me of a small, gray field mouse lost in the vast, empty room. There were going to be speeches on the account of Comrade Stalin, and our principal, Mr. Zalewski said we should grieve. I didn't know how, but Sophie probably would, I thought. We were dismissed right after the morning assembly and reminded about the three minutes of silence in memory of Comrade Stalin, which the whole world was going to observe at ten o'clock. The idea of the whole world coming to a standstill at the same time for three minutes sounded, indeed, intriguing. Cars not driving, people not walking, the daily business of living interrupted, suspended on orders from someone—someone who had the awesome power to do it. We were even told not to talk during these three minutes. So my attention was divided between the unexpected arrival of Sophie and the events connected with the unexpected departure of Comrade Stalin.

Our class was dismissed well before ten o'clock. I patiently waited by the main door, as always, for Sophie to appear so that we could finally be together. Outside, the snow mixed with rain fell steadily between the gusts of wind, which were short but powerful. Sophie appeared at the end of the hall, walking slowly, hesitantly toward me. "Hurry up!" I yelled. "I've got an umbrella!"

Next, we were out in the street, huddled under my dad's big, black umbrella, just like we used to. When the time came for the three minutes for Comrade Stalin, it was grand, I thought.

The sirens went on in the factories all over town, the streetcars stopped and rang their bells, buses and cars came to rest in the middle of the streets. Only people ignored the whole thing. People kept walking, talking, and entering stores, shopping for potatoes and carrots at vegetable stands. I wanted to do as they did, to defy, to disobey, so I pulled on Sophie to go, but she wouldn't budge. She was trembling, tears streaming down her face, looking at the oversized portrait of Comrade Stalin that was hastily hung over the entrance to the post office and adorned across the corner with a piece of black cloth. She was attracting attention of the people passing by. They either looked at her, bewildered, or made some mean or nasty remarks. I suddenly felt the need to protect her, save her. Again she reminded me of a small field mouse, lost, sensing for direction.

An old woman in a brown coat was approaching us, carrying her groceries in a canvas bag. Her thin, tight lips formed an ugly, malicious grimace. Something awful was about to happen, but I was stricken, unable to move. The woman came up to Sophie and looked at her face, wet with rain and tears, chin quivering uncontrollably, eyes fixed on Comrade Stalin. She crossed herself and then she spat on Sophie's cheek.

The Tapeworm

"…and what does your father do for a living?"

Mrs. Anna Pawlak looked up from her notebook filled with columns of fine, black squiggles. The only remaining blank space was next to my name.

"Agnes," she said again softly, "surely you know what your father does for a living."

I felt my cheeks turn crimson; I intently studied my shoes.

Anna Pawlak was not mean. She was not trying to hurt me or embarrass me. The truth was I didn't know what my father did. At that moment I wished he did something terribly simple like baking bread, laying bricks, driving a bus. I wished I could have summed up his being in one word: a builder, a miner, a shoemaker, a…anything. I didn't know what he was, and I suspect, at the time, neither did he.

I suddenly remembered something he recently said when the subject of money came up in our house, so I whispered to redeem myself in Mrs. Pawlak's eyes, to vindicate him, and to get her attention. "Mrs. Pawlak, now I remember something. I think he is looking for opportunities."

Mrs. Pawlak gazed at me and said nothing.

Father seemed to have found the opportunity he was looking for that very year, early in the spring. I was doing homework on the floor of the dining room when I heard him telling Mother that everything was going to change. I moved my books closer to the door to listen. I was not about to be caught by surprise.

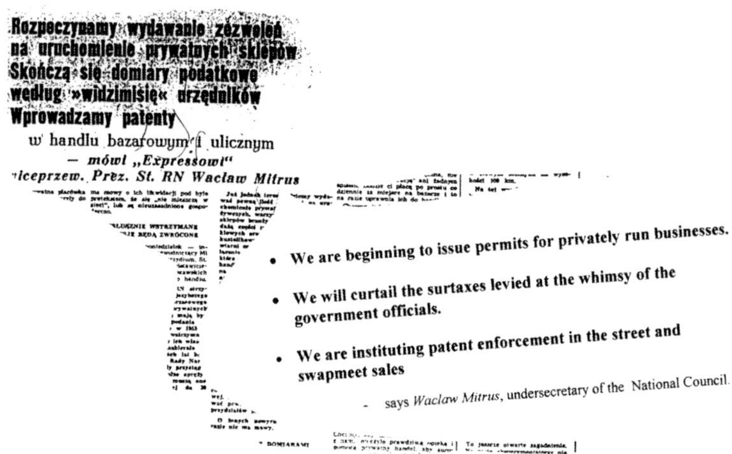

"I'm telling you, Janie, there is a thaw underway in the party," he was saying. "The papers call it 'the economic renewal.' Plain citizens like us will be able to organize into collectives—no, no"—he pulled the newspaper out of the pocket of his coat and pointed to the front page—"here it is, *cooperatives*—and contribute to the growth of our socialist economy and you know whatever the papers print has to have party's blessing." *What's got into him?* I thought. The way he talked was weird. He was going to get Uncle Bert, Fishel, Pan Stasio, and Pan Przemek, and some "other guys" and start this cooperative thing. Mama, during his speech, was peeling potatoes over the sink.

"What will you do with the cooperative once you have started it?" she asked without as much as turning around.

"We'll get all the necessary papers and permits, and then we'll make something small and simple that people will buy. People need just about everything. They'll buy just about anything."

"Something small and simple," Mama repeated. "Like buttons?"

"Yeah, like buttons!" he cried. "That's a great idea." He was excited, I could tell.

For awhile after that, he left the house early in the morning and came back late at night. In the evening he spoke very little and picked at his dinner. He was nervous and looked tired. One evening he came home with vodka on his breath.

"I know you didn't believe me, Janie," he said to Mama. "But we did it! We have the permits, the machine is in place, and we have the plastic pellets. We will be making buttons and plastic combs and selling them to government stores! Co-op number one-three-four is on its way!" he cried, and with a gesture of a magician pulling a rabbit from under his coat, he produced a bottle of Russian brandy.

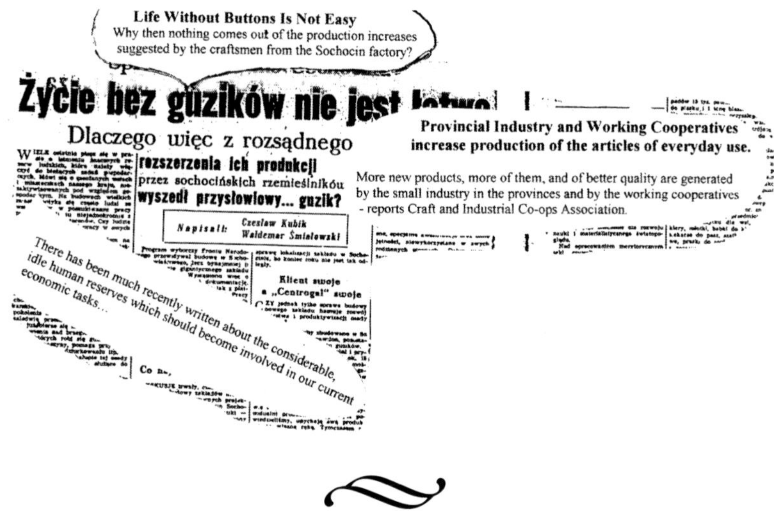

A thin, violet ribbon of smoke was rising from the pile of dry leaves on the brown lawn in front of the building at 8a Styki

Street. The smoke spiraled then lightly dipped, doubled over itself, and again changed direction. A small, orange flame was skipping upon the top of the leaves, which shrunk, turned gray, and fell apart into tiny glowing particles. I liked the penetrating, sour odor of rotting leaves and freshly uncovered earth mixed with the smell of smoke.

It was December 4th, 1953, the Coal Miners' Day—another working-class holiday. Schools were closed, and I didn't quite know what to do with myself, having all that time on my hands. *If there had been snow*, I thought longingly, *I would be out with my sled, on the dike by the river.* Instead, I was leaning against the gate to our apartment building, watching Pan Konstanty Galazka, who, with broad, sweeping motions, was raking the rest of the leaves into the burning pile. He was the janitor at building 8a.

While I was looking at him, it occurred to me that last night he had probably slept on his left side. On that side his dark hair was flatly stuck to his skull while on the top, it stood straight up in small, greasy clumps. From the corner of his mouth hung a cigarette butt. From time to time, Pan Galazka gracefully flipped it up with a small motion of his upper lip, to take a puff, and then let it fall again. After a repeated display of this extraordinary skill, Pan Galazka took the butt delicately in his yellowed fingers, released from his lungs a cloud of gray smoke, and said, "It's going to snow; you'll see, Miss. Before dinnertime you'll have your snow."

The clouds hung very low, heavy under the weight of their white burden. It seemed to me that everyone must have been waiting for the snow as anxiously as I had. When the city was covered even with a thin layer of snow, the sight of it was bearable. Under the snow it looked whole, clean, and unreal. Every year I longed for the snow to come.

When the flakes began to fall, they were large and flat like the wafers the priest gave out during the Holy Communion. Father came out of the stairwell with a gray fedora in his hand. Before he had time to put it on, a few of the white wafers fell on his dark hair.

"Well, here is your snow, princess. Are you all happy now?"

I nodded, and he took my hand. "Today your mama sends us off to work together. There's nothing for you to do here," he said.

We started for the bus stop. It wasn't often that Father and I were alone together like this. Even though I had a hard time figuring what he was, I liked being with him. I liked when he took me with him. Things, interesting things, seemed to happen when he was around, and it made me feel good holding his hand. On the bus everyone smelled of cigarettes and mothballs, and I liked that also. After all, he smelled that way too.

We walked hand in hand down Sienna Street among the ruins of buildings, bombed and burned either by Germans or Russians—I never quite remembered which. The ruins were just objects in a landscape I was born into and grew up in. They were very appealing to the imagination and served as excellent playground for all sorts of games. Many grownups I knew, like Grandma T., Pan Przemek, and even Father, were very emotional about what the ruins were before they became ruins, but it seemed to have happened long before I was born, and I felt had nothing to do with me. A thin layer of snow had already covered the sidewalk and piles of bricks and garbage. Snow hung on cornices and windowsills, which framed black, gaping openings into nonexistent apartments. A white layer lined the remnant of stairs leading to nowhere.

Co-op No.134 consisted of a large lot surrounded by a wooden fence made of old, blackened boards and a rectangular, dilapidated barrack, which was put together from the same material. On the left side of the lot, next to a shed grandly named the "tool house," an old wreck of a Soviet semi from WWII rested upon a pile of rubble. It had no wheels or doors, and it leaned slightly to one side. Because of the rains, the lot was usually a large, muddy bog where safe paths were marked by the boards torn from the fence and supported on bricks.

A small, wooden outhouse was haphazardly attached to the side of the barrack, which was close to the center of the lot. Behind it, from the barrack wall emerged a pipe secured at the other end to a metal stove, called, for some unexplained reason, "the goat." The smoke rising from this pipe in winter caused the outhouse to appear suspended in the clouds, a mystic center of this surreal landscape.

When I first visited Co-op No.134, I was excitedly expecting to see father's great machine spitting out shiny buttons and combs. Instead I found it cold and dormant in the corner of the barrack. What my father and his partners did in the Co-op No.134 had once again become difficult for me to define. Most frequently I saw them gathered around the table, under the cold light of a naked bulb. They smoked, played cards, and drank vodka for warmth. I presided in the corner at an old desk. I drew and cut out dolls and used official stamps of the co-op, but most of all, I listened to the conversations. They usually concerned matters that took place in a very distant past, which for me was before the war, or a bit more recently, during the war. Listening to these tales, it seemed to me that all the interesting and important things had already taken place in the past and that the present was not worth the trouble. It existed only as an illusion, something tacitly agreed upon.

Sometimes a bell at the gate rang, and then Father would say to Fishel, "Go see who it is—but take it easy; don't rush."

I liked Fishel a lot. He was dark and small, and his movements were abrupt but nimble. He reminded me of a brown ferret I once saw. He seemed to be a lot younger than the rest of the men. We got to know each other because Fishel never drank, and when the others did, he often left the card table to boil water for tea in the banged-up, aluminum kettle. Sometimes waiting for the water to boil, he sat at the desk across from me and pulled out a book. When I asked him what it was about, he usually abandoned the reading willingly to tell me the story of Madam Bovary or Anna Karenina.

Whenever Fishel went to the gate to check out the "customer," the remaining men crowded around the two small windows facing the gate. The early identification of the customer, while Fishel still led him or her through the path of boards resting above the mud, seemed to be an important part of the ritual. The majority of the customers carried suitcases or large travel bags. After my first few visits to Co-op No.134, I began to suspect that something deeply mysterious was going on there and that it had nothing to do with making either buttons or plastic combs. When a stranger with a suitcase came while I was there, my father immediately, under some silly pretext, sent me outside to play.

On the day the snow fell, Fishel brought a tall, stout woman from the gate with a bright red nose and cheeks. She wore a black coat, as big as a tent, and held two large baskets. Father leaned across the table and whispered, "Fishel, take the kid outside." Fishel got my coat. He helped me with the buttons, because everyone was waiting for me to go, and then he gently pushed me toward the door.

"Clear out, princess," he said. "Go, play war in the truck or… something."

The big woman smiled at me with the corners of her mouth, which prompted me to resist.

"But it's so cold out there," I argued. "I may get pneumonia, and it will be your fault."

Fishel wasn't buying it, and he continued to maneuver me to the exit.

"It's better to go, better not to know," he sung softly into my ear. "Be off, your highness," he added louder, opening the door for me with a deep bow.

Right then Pan Przemek, one of my father's card partners, took pity on me and said, "Go with the kid, Fishel. Show her Stasio's tapeworm. It must be already frozen stiff out there, since yesterday."

I eagerly followed Fishel upon the snow-covered planks across the lot. The tapeworm had piqued my curiosity. It was a creature known to me primarily from my mother's grisly tales. She occasionally called upon it to scare off my father from eating pork chops and roasts at the state-run cafeterias and other public eateries. Every time Father declined to eat dinner after coming home in the evening, Mama conducted an investigation. If it turned out that he had grabbed something while in town, I immediately imagined a slimy, snake-like animal impudently prowling my father's bowels.

"Why did Pan Przemek say that the tapeworm belongs to Pan Stasio?" I asked.

"Because it came out of Pan Stasio," said Fishel, skillfully balancing on the iced-over plank while my legs were sliding and slipping in all directions.

"It came out on its own, just like that?" I inquired. We stopped in the middle of the plank, and I stared at Fishel in disbelief.

"Well…not quite on its own," he said. "What chased it out was, probably, a fair amount of vodka mixed with a few shots of cordial, followed by a beer chaser, and then your father's own, homemade concoction of vodka and green walnut juice."

"You mean it's like my father inventing a tapeworm medicine?"

"Well…not quite. Because, I suspect, Pan Tapeworm was, at that point, probably as drunk as Pan Stasio and simply took a wrong turn, or maybe it just has had enough and wanted to catch a breath of fresh air. It all could have been just a case of bad timing." Fishel took my hand and pulled me behind him. Again we started moving slowly along the planks toward the wreck.

"What does 'bad timing' mean?" I was impatiently shaking Fishel's large hand holding mine.

"Well…it happened when Pan Stasio went to the outhouse. I mean, the tapeworm, it started coming out. So Stasio begun to holler, and we all ran to see it. When he let us into the outhouse, the tapeworm was already down there, you know. Then your dad got us some wire, and we fished the beast out. We spread it on the wreck to see how long it really was." I jerked Fishel's hand, and again we came to a dead stop in the middle of the plank.

"And it is still there, spread on the truck?"

"Yeah, it's still there…" Suddenly Fishel shivered. "Come on, princess. Now I'll get the pneumonia."

I wasn't sure what to expect, but neither Fishel nor I were prepared for what awaited us. The sight of the tapeworm draped over the snow-covered wreck was unimaginably beautiful. The generous white layer rounded and smoothed out all the rough angles, and the wreck appeared like a great, white, modern sculpture I had seen in the museum picture books. Silky, white, and delicate, the tapeworm garland fell in one soft swoop from the front reflector and then rose to the top of the fender and then again down to the cab step and up onto its roof. Then it came to rest on the exposed back axle. It was sparkling, iridescent, and narrow like a ribbon. Here and there, a few small snowflakes rested on its surface and reflected the light, magically magnifying the shimmering effect. Fishel and I stood motionless, in silent awe, contemplating the transfiguration of the tapeworm and the wreck into a thing of strange beauty, a white marble upon which, in places, a small light was restlessly dancing.

I slipped on the iced-over board and fell, hitting the middle of the tapeworm garland, pulling Fishel behind me. He tumbled onto the snow-covered fender. Under his weight, the fender separated from the wreck, and in its place there remained a great, black, gaping wound. The frozen tapeworm shattered into hundreds of tiny pieces, which disappeared in the thick white cover on the ground. The snow continued to fall silently.

Fishel cut his hand on the rusty edge of the fender. Stepping carefully, I followed him back to the barrack. Drops of blood fell from his hand and, just like the tapeworm crystals, disappeared without a trace into the mass of delicate white feathers.

Inside everything was back to normal. The big lady was gone. On the table, there was a deck of old cards and, as usual, a half-finished bottle.

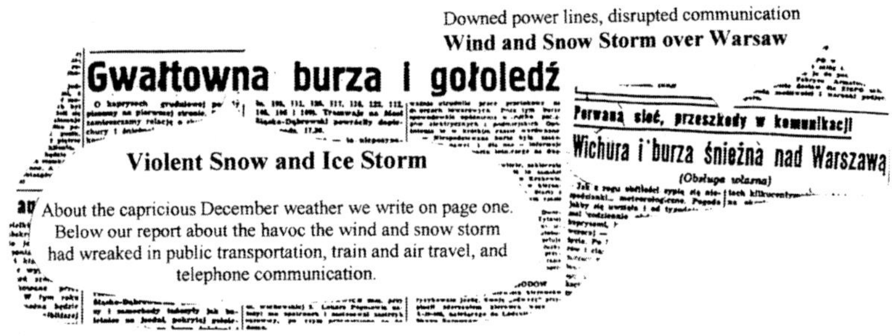

"Let's break it up for today, gentlemen, or we'll be snowed in here for good," said my father. "Bundle up and put your gloves on, princess. Let's see if we can get us a cab."

But it was already too late. Even buses and trams stranded in the roadway at different points of the city were abandoned. The whole city, as a matter of fact, came to a halt because of the snow, which kept falling and falling. Father held my hand tightly and pulled me behind him. The snow on the sidewalk was over his ankles and almost up to my knees. We made slow headway toward a larger street where there was still some traffic. In the middle of the roadway, completely covered with snow, a few cars danced strange rumbas, swinging their trunks to the left then to the right.

"It doesn't look like we're going to get that cab anytime soon," said Father. "Are you very cold, princess?" I was fine except for my feet. The snow got inside my shoes while we were walking, but I wasn't about to tell him that. As long as I was with him, cold feet or not, I was all right. A few minutes later one of the slipping cars stopped in front of us. The driver felt sorry for me and for fifty *zlotys* was ready to take us at least part of the way. He let us off at the far side of the Red Army Plaza. We had to continue for the rest of the way on foot. Father was happy that the end of the trip was in sight. He must have guessed the truth about my feet.

Among the buildings on Paryska Street, it was quiet. We were walking in the middle of the roadway. The black fingers of the trees growing on both sides of the street came together above our heads, and the snow didn't fall as heavily. The flakes were smaller and spun lightly in the air as if they had come from a giant, rotating sieve. It was an early, winter dusk. The outlines of buildings, trees, cars, and people gradually became blurred, wrapped in a pearl-gray mist. When we turned into our street, I noticed two cars parked in front of building 8a, the domain of Pan Galazka. They were completely covered with snow and looked like two humps of a monstrous camel.

In the stairwell of our building, we stopped to shake off our coats and shoes. Father took off his hat. There were a good three centimeters of snow on its rim. We made our way up the stairs in the dark. Father said that the fuse was probably blown again. I heard him swear softly under his breath.

He was searching for his keys when the door to our apartment opened. A stranger stood in the doorway. He was tall and completely bald, wore high leather boots, and a dark gray jacket. An eerie silence fell over the threshold, during which, in the dark, Father's hand found mine. He held it tight, very tight, and this rigid tightness traveled all the way from my hand to my heart.

I nervously followed Father's gaze. He was looking at the mirror, crookedly hanging in the hallway, behind the stranger's back. In the mirror I could see Uncle Henry and another man sitting around the table. The man was talking to Uncle Henry, and, at the same time, he was writing something on the piece of paper in front of him. In the armchair, next to the desk, sat a militiaman wearing a uniform. I recognized him as Pan Wladek who occasionally played cards with my father. He came about once every month, played cards, drank some vodka, and always collected two hundred *zlotys* from my father, whether he won or lost. I wondered about the game they played and why my father always seemed to lose. Now, Pan Wladek was going through the papers in the drawer of Father's desk. Still another man was standing next to the window, watching the street through the crack in the shutters.

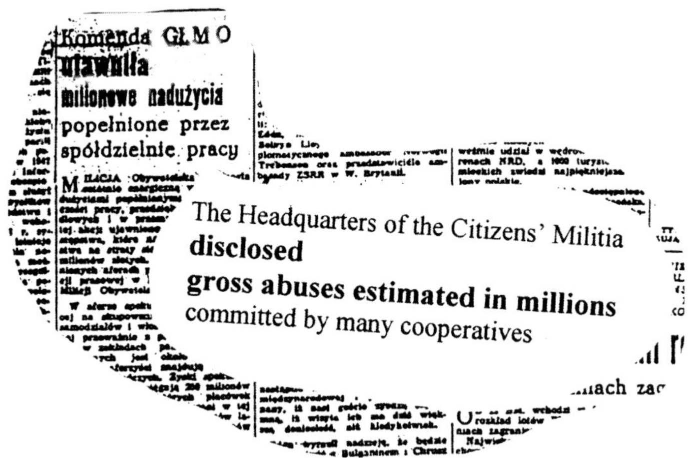

Suddenly Mama appeared in the mirror, carrying a shoebox full of old letters and an armful of picture albums in which she had been meticulously arranging our family photos. Behind Mama there was a man in a green shirt, buttoned all the way up. When Mama saw that the entry door was open, her face became the color of the burning leaves, and her hands fell along the sides of her body. The silence was shattered by the noise of the albums and letters crashing onto the table and the floor. Father still held my hand and I felt a leaning of his body, a sudden readiness to step forward. But he didn't.

Mama stood in midst of the letters and photographs scattered on the floor when the man who opened the door for us said, "Pan Korsak?…and this must be Miss Agnes. Please do come in. We have been waiting for you here, for quite a while."

The Map of America

When I think of Roman Wyglondalo, goose bumps appear on my upper arms, and my elbows begin to itch, just the way they did when I knew him. I was afraid of him then, and with good reason. He hated my guts. His dislike of me must have sprung from the fact that his mother did our laundry, and he was ashamed of it. He had said himself that what she did was "tend to other people's dirt."

Mama knew Mrs. Wyglondalo from long before the war and always meticulously put away money in order to pay Mrs. Wyglondalo for washing our stuff once a month. After the security men took away father and Uncle Bert and closed the co-op, we had very little money except what Uncle Henry and Fishel gave to us. From time to time Fishel also brought us eggs and chickens, which Mama said he probably stole somewhere. But I didn't believe it. I knew she was just teasing him this way. During that time Mama and I washed all the small pieces ourselves, and Mrs. W. came to help us do the linens and towels. She didn't want to take any money.

It was hard to tell how old Mrs. W. really was. She couldn't have been much older than Mama, but she was all dried up and warped. The skin on her face was like Mama's old leather purse, brownish and full of creases and folds. Her hands reminded me of the roots of an old birch growing in the courtyard that here and there stuck out from the dirt. I could never get a good look at her legs, even when she bent over the tub, because her skirts were too long and revealed only a pair of crooked and worn brown shoes. I wanted to see her legs because of the way she walked, slowly shifting the weight from side to side. I suspected she had either short stilts or wooden feet. She was always warm and smelled of soap. She seemed content, or at least at peace with herself, and probably looked upon Mama's attempts to master the art of squeezing the soapy water out of the enormous wet sheets as a temporary aberration.

She often spoke of Roman. She said he was handsome and very smart, and I had a feeling Mrs. W. was exceedingly proud of him. Roman was one of the most gifted students. Roman studied a lot and read those thick, heavy books. Roman was very busy because Mr. Zalewski, the school principal, relied on Roman to do things for him. That was what Mrs. W. talked about all the time.

This was before Father and Uncle Bert were taken away, when they were still busy with the co-op and Father was coming home late in the evenings. On the day when Mrs. W. was doing father's shirts, Mama decided to ask Mrs. W. and Roman to eat dinner with us. Mrs. W. wrote a note to Roman. She laboriously chiseled the large, childish letters into the paper, and then she handed it to me.

Mrs. W. lived just a few blocks away, and from the directions she gave me, I knew what building she meant. It was one of the structures Mama had warned me, time after time, not to enter under any circumstances. The upper floors of the building were blown away by a bomb, and what remained was a part of the stairwell, the floor of the first level, and the basement. There were still many sites of this sort around the city, and they were children's favorite playgrounds. The bizarre setting had an irresistible appeal. It was sometime ago that Mother summoned me to the kitchen stool and instructed me as to the dangers that lurked there. She had me make a list of all the terrible things she said might happen to me, and she pinned it with a large safety pin to the lampshade next to my bed. I was expected to review this list immediately after waking up and right before going to bed:

1. The walls and floors might be unstable and collapse on my head.

2. In the rubble, unexploded shells might still be buried, waiting to blow me to bits.

3. Gypsies might be hiding there and kidnap me to Romania.

It made me very uneasy that now, with Mama's permission, Mrs. W. was sending me off to the once-forbidden territory.

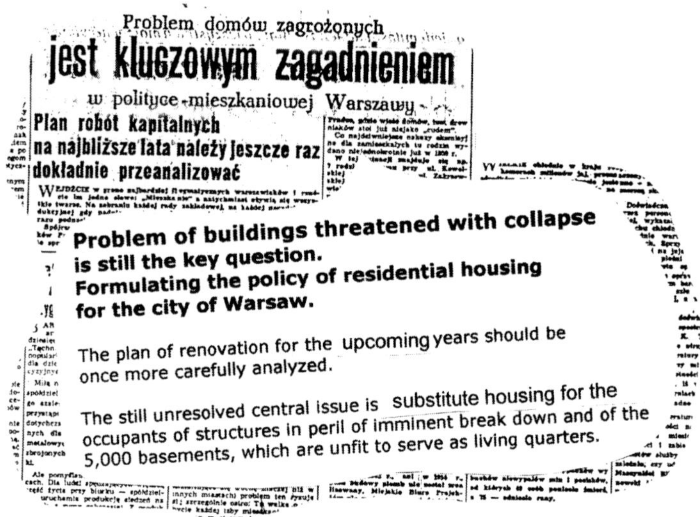

Problem of buildings threatened with collapse is still the key question. Formulating the policy of residential housing for the city of Warsaw.

The plan of renovation for the upcoming years should be once more carefully analyzed.

The still unresolved central issue is substitute housing for the occupants of structures in peril of imminent break down and of the 5,000 basements, which are unfit to serve as living quarters.

Before entering, I looked over Mrs. W's building one more time. Only part of one wall, about two stories high, remained of the entire structure. I stood in the opening that used to be the main entrance to the stairwell. Above was a solid gray sky, and chunks of concrete hung on twisted, metal rods jutting from its upper part. To the right, a few steps led to what once was the first floor, and to the left, steps descended into the dark bowels of the cellar. I stood at the top for awhile, scratching my elbows through the sleeves of my winter coat, trying to make up my mind to go down, when I heard someone coughing. Step by step, I felt my way until I saw a thin line of yellow light coming from under the door. A musty, putrid odor hung heavily in the still air. My feet became entangled in a rag at the threshold. I lost balance, and I knocked my head against the door. Just then someone called out, "It's open."

There was no one in the first room, but then the same voice said, "I'm in here," and I followed it through the doorless opening to another room. On a rusty, iron bed a boy was lying on his stomach, reading a book by the light of a small lamp. He had dark curly hair, which fell on his forehead and into his eyes. They were black and glistening like tar. The light from the lamp was swimming on their surface. He was annoyed at me for interrupting.

"What do you want?" he asked impatiently.

"Your mama is doing our wash," I said. "She wants you to come eat dinner at our place. Here." I handed him the note and waited while he read. He looked familiar, but there was not enough light in the room to get a really good look at his face. The room was like a tomb—it had no windows.

"What are you waiting for?" he cried angrily, his eyes full of loathing.

I guess I expected him to say yes or no or some sort of an excuse, but instead he hissed through his teeth, "Get out! And stop snooping around!"

On my way out, I looked over the first room. This one had a window, but in spite of it, the rancid, nauseating smell was more pervasive here. Way up near the ceiling, there was this opening about four feet wide and three feet high. It had five thick, vertical, metal bars. This is how, later on, I always imagined the prison cell where Father and Uncle Bert were locked up for whatever they were doing at the co-op 134. After a few brief visits there, even I could tell they were not making any combs or buttons they were supposed to make to begin with. I know that at the start they were trying to make them because I saw those buttons with my own eyes when Mama took out her sewing machine and out of an old sheet fashioned tiny bags for each 100 of them. She had me sort them out into piles of three different sizes, and then into still smaller piles, counting off 100 buttons into each pile. But what happened to them later was a mystery. One of those mysteries you wondered about but knew better than to ask.

This room not only stuck in my mind as the closest thing to a prison cell, there was one other odd thing about it. One of the walls was covered with two blankets sewn together. They hung about ten centimeters away from its surface, not flat against it.

There was something behind them, something meant to be hidden from view. I hesitated for a moment, wanting to take a peek, but *Stop snooping around!* still rang in my ears. I was afraid of Roman Wyglondalo.

Later, the same afternoon he came to dinner directly from the meeting of the school's Socialist Youth Organization. He was much taller than I expected after our earlier encounter in his cellar. He looked very handsome, indeed, in a black open jacket over the starched white shirt and bright red cravat. I brought him to the table where Mama was arranging plates and flatware. Just about that time Mrs. W. also came up from our cellar where she had spent the day among the tubs and buckets of soapy water. When she saw Roman decked out in red and white, she became embarrassed and pulled him aside. She began to admonish him in loud whisper:

"Take it off! Take it off right now!" She was tugging at his crimson necktie. "I won't have you offending these good people in their own home!"

Roman's face became the color of his neckwear. All he managed to say through his clenched teeth was, "Mama, stop, please…stop." Then, in desperation, he quickly pulled his tie off, rolled it up, and stuffed it into his pocket. He sat at the dinner table in his open shirt, relegated to being the son of the woman who "tended to other people's dirt." He was pale and chewed nervously on his lower lip. In one short glance, he told me how much he hated me for being a witness to his humiliation. The intensity of his glance made me go for my elbows again, and above them I felt the rough tips of goose bumps.

During that dinner I realized I had seen Roman earlier, much earlier. It was at school. I had not seen much of him because he was a few years older than I. He was graduating that year while I was only in sixth grade. But I remembered him well enough, greeting local party officials who always came to school to celebrate anniversaries of the October Revolution or of the great victory over the Nazis. Tall, handsome, important, and wearing the red tie. Despite his evident dislike, I was quite ready to worship him. That evening, after dinner I was also ready to join the Socialist Youth Organization. First because he was one of its outstanding members, and second because I liked red ties.

The following day Father came home late from the co-op, and Mama was heating pork chops for him while he read his paper at the table. The newspaper was an important part of his evening ritual. It shielded him from Mama's daily problems and her small complaints and also provided topics for lively discussions with Uncle Bert, Uncle Henry, Pan Przemek, Pan Janek Gorko, and Fishel. At the onset of these debates all, including Father, always agreed that the paper was lying. Then they concentrated on determining if there was at least a little bit of truth to what was reported, and if so, what did this grain of truth meant to us. How would it influence our lives? Let's say there was news about North Korean Freedom Fighters lead by Ho Szi Min initiating the spring offensive. First of all it was doubtful it was an offensive at all. More likely a small skirmish, on the outskirts of some godforsaken hamlet deep in a tropical jungle. But for us here, did these mean shortages of rice in grocery stores? Prices of coal going up before winter? To Father the paper was a lifeline that connected us to a larger world, the world beyond the Iron Curtain. This phrase was usually spoken in a hushed voice and was a cue for me to gather my homework and move to the kitchen table. But this evening there were just the three of us at home, and I sat across from him with a pencil and an empty piece of paper. I was planning to draw from memory a portrait of Roman, wearing his red tie. I had prepared a red crayon for this purpose.

"What is the Socialist Youth Organization?" I asked.

"Sort of a new Hitler *Jugend*," my father informed me from behind the paper.

I was about to ask what "Hitler *Jugend*" was when Mama intervened: "Now, Theo, what kind of answer it this to a twelve-year-old? Do you want her to go out and repeat it? Eat your pork chops, and mind your tongue, if you please." I knew he must have goofed because Mama was upset.

She turned to me and said, "The Socialist Youth Organization is for the young people who, when they grow up, want to become communist party members. Why do you want to know?" she asked.

I was fiddling with the red crayon to delay the answer. I remembered Mrs. W's reaction to Roman's red tie. Something in me wanted to put my parents to a test, and, besides, I knew that the truth was not going to go over too well.

"I heard they have summer camp at Mazury Lakes every year," I ventured cautiously. "I thought I might sign up before the school is out."

Pregnant silence descended upon us. The newspaper was slowly lowered, revealing my father's face. For a moment he looked steadily at Mama and then disappeared again behind the columns of print. After exchanging glances with Father, Mama turned to me. Under her gaze the silence began to condense on my forehead into tiny pearls of moisture.

"Now, you are too young, Aggie," she finally said. "You have to be in high school to join. So it's good you still have some months to think about it. Think how many grownups you know who are members of the party and also how many of your friends want to join ZMP and go to this camp. When you count both, come and talk to me about it."

Suddenly I felt as if someone had lifted an odd weight off my shoulders that I, unwittingly, placed there myself. It was the first time I was really glad to be too young for something.

Every spring I used to stand still, close my eyelids, and raise my face to the sun. Through my eyelids, I could still see the light. I would put my face to the sun like a radar dish to gather up all the timid rays, to soak them up like a sponge. In March the world still hibernated in a deep freeze. Then on April third, the spring sort of exploded. In a few days, pale-green clouds hovered over the poplars and chestnuts, and robins screamed in the half-bare lilacs under the window, keeping us up at night. It was our first spring without Father.

I stood in the courtyard of our building with my face up, watching the sun through my eyelids. "What on earth are you doing there, Agnes?" I heard Mama's voice above me. She was leaning out the window of our apartment. "Hurry up; I need the cream to make the dumplings. Fishel is coming for dinner. And don't forget about Mrs. Wyglondalo. Where is the pitcher I gave you for the cream?"

I reluctantly opened my eyes and could see the sun no longer. If I tried to explain what exactly I was doing, it would probably take a while, so I just waved the blue pitcher toward Mama and without a word skipped out of her sight.

Before I bought a quarter of a liter of cream for the dumplings, I was to take a message to Mrs. Wyglondalo. The message was simple enough: Mama wanted to know if she could do our drapes and table linens before Easter. However, I was very unsure about its delivery. On the way to Mrs. Wyglondalo's place, I imagined several scenarios that did not call for me to go down into the smelly dungeon and face the ugly beast, who really was a handsome prince. I was still standing in front of the place, meditating how to deliver Mama's message, when I noticed beyond the mounds of dirt, scattered bricks, and sprouting weeds, the upper part of the window to the first room of Mrs. Wyglondalo's apartment. Through this window I could talk to Mrs. Wyglondalo and get the matter settled.

The window was open, and I could see the light in the room although it was a sunny day and early in the afternoon. The ledge was but twenty centimeters off the ground. I had to crouch to look inside. The door to the room was also open, and I felt a draft blowing through the room. Two metal desk lamps were standing on the wooden bench placed along the wall, which earlier had been covered by the hanging blankets. Now the blankets were removed, and the stream of light from the lamps was directed at the exposed wall. What I saw on its surface was a large and very strange painting indeed. It was done in muted, dirty tones. In the middle spread a wide, mustard-colored plane, which, to the left, gradually darkened into a brown and muddy-purple ridge. There the plaster swelled, buckled, and cracked. In the cracks, drops of moisture glistened in the light like ice. Toward the bottom, on the left side, the water, which oozed from the purple mounds and trickled down the wall, formed a finger-like yellow stain. I knelt down and pressed my head between the metal bars to get a better look. Taking in every detail of the secret painting, I quite forgot about Mrs. Wyglondalo, cream for the dumplings, and the blue jar Mama had given me.

On the right side, the mustard plane gradually took on pale-green tones, gaining in intensity toward its outer edge. A dark, bottle green thumb jutted out from the colorful mass pointing directly to the door leading to the next room. At first the entire painting appeared to me as a giant hand closing upon the grayness of the wall with a thin pinky-finger sticking out on the left. Then my geography class flashed in my mind. The enormous pull-down maps of all the parts of the world: Europe, Asia,

Africa, and finally North America. Yes! Yes! It was the map of North America!

"And who do we have here? It's the little shithead, no doubt, with her dirty laundry," I recognized Roman's voice. He was standing in the doorway to the other room. Frantically I pushed away from the metal bars in the window, wanting to get up and run, but my head was stuck between them. At that moment I was willing to have my ears cut off if only I could free myself from the damned window. When Roman realized my predicament, he began laughing hysterically and repeating, "You're stuck! The shithead is stuck! Ha, ha, ha! Look at that! The shithead is stuck!"

Stricken with terror, I tried to force my head between the bars, tearing off the skin behind my ears in the process. My painful efforts were punctuated with Roman's fits of laughter.

"Die and rot there forever, shithead." He pronounced this sentence upon me in a deep, suddenly serious voice. He then turned off the lights and slammed the door behind him. I listened for his footsteps up the staircase and on the side of the building. It didn't take a great strategist to realize how vulnerable my position really was. My front was pinned, for all practical purposes immobilized, while my flanks and rear were dangerously exposed. He came around from the back and delivered one swift, well-aimed kick at my butt, another one at Mama's blue cream pitcher. Then he left without a word.

I sat on the ground with my head between the bars, crying more on the account of my injured pride than because of my injured ears and aching behind. Mama came looking for me in about an hour. My embarrassment was compounded by her failure to free me from the window in spite of undoing my braids and trying to push my head through with hair down, covering my ears. She ran home and stuck the note in our door for Fishel to come immediately to Mrs. Wyglondalo. He came but had no tools. Mr. Galazka, the janitor at the building next door to ours, came too, summoned by Fishel. He was equipped with a large piece of iron rail. They were followed by a large group of kids that played in the street at the time. It all turned into a rescue on a grand scale, with Mr. Galazka sliding the rail under my chin, Fishel holding the rag, which isolated it from my flesh, Mama worrying aloud about the safety of my entire head, and a gathering of kids and bystanders watching, commenting, advising, and in the end cheering when Mr. Galazka pried the bars apart and my head was freed without further damage to my ears. Mama and Fishel both hugged me as if I were rescued from a burning house.

"Why in the world did you stick your head in there, princess?" asked Fishel.

"I wanted to see the map of America," I said.

"A whaaat?" Mama and Fishel sang out in unison.

Although Mama explained to me that it was no map of America but moisture seeping through the wall, bringing with it probably some sewer water (which would account for the awful stench) and decomposing debris, upon which mold, mildew, and fungi of various types were growing, I deeply believed it was some wonderful kind of magic that it all came together to form a map of America. The map itself and the circumstances of its discovery were all much too exciting to keep to myself. I could not help but share it first with Sophie and then at school with Magda and Maggie, the Zycer twins. I even pointed Roman out to them during the long break while he was playing soccer with the older boys. The girls agreed that he was exceptionally handsome. "Like Gerard Philipe," said Magda Zycer, turning her eyes heavenward.

The next day she whispered to me that she too had seen the map of America. Her sister Maggie said she was lying because last night when they went to Roman's building, the light in the basement was turned off, and they couldn't see anything. Still

Magda insisted that she saw the map even in the dark. Two other kids who had gone with them said they also saw something on the wall that looked like a map, so Magda pushed Maggie against the chain link fence, and Maggie spat on her just as the bell rung at the end of the break.

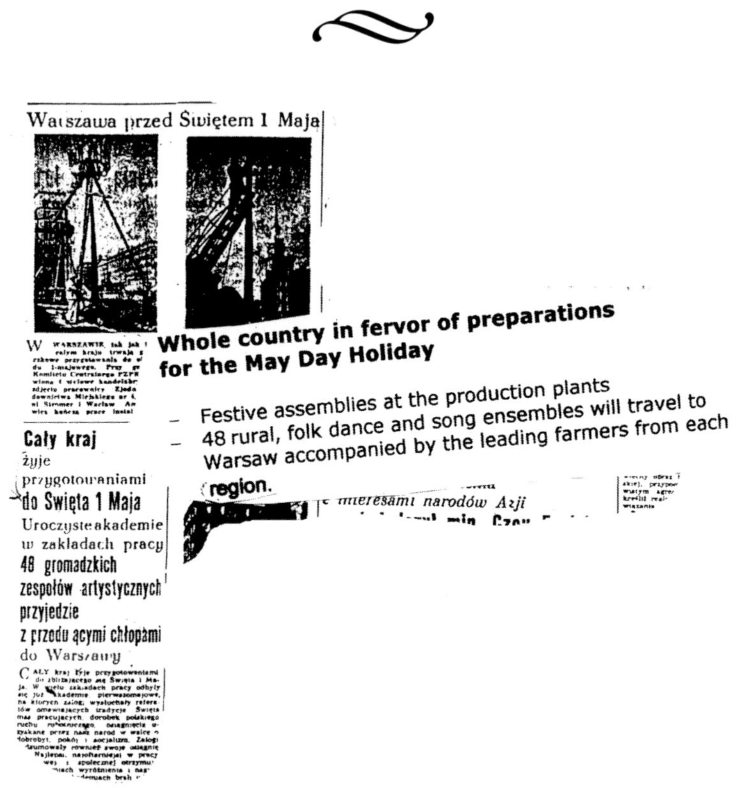

I was tired of marching up and down the soccer field. Up and down, across and back, and up and down again. I was bored and tired and hungry. Mr. Zalewski had us marching for hours every day after school. We were getting ready for the great proletarian holiday—the May Day Parade. Last year, on the account of Comrade Stalin's passing, the celebration was somewhat subdued, but this year we were going all out. The front page of the paper that like clock work appeared every day on our table in the big room had pictures and articles about the whole nation getting ready for the May Day Holiday. The parade route was being decorated, and portraits of leaders and "laureates of the Stalin's Award and other representatives of the progressive tradition" were being hung along the way. I wondered since Father was gone, who was reading the paper?

Our school was going to march, led by the members of the school's Socialist Youth Organization. Roman was usually at the head of the column, and watching him, talking about him, and giggling were welcomed distractions. Today, however, he was absent for some reason, and our PE teacher, Mr. Siwek, was carrying the red flag with the number of the organization's cell and the name of our school on it. Long red and white ribbons attached to the top of the flag flapped in the wind, and we followed, carrying portraits of Comrade Stalin, Comrade Lenin, and other comrades and singing hymns about our fatherland, the party, and workers uniting for the march.

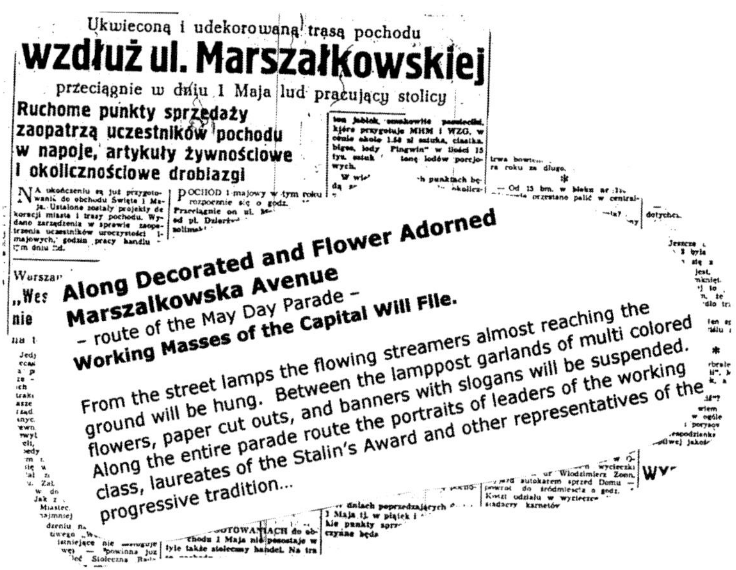

It was much like the church processions winding around the churchyard. Banners with ribbons and images of saints and hymn singing too. For the church processions, Mama had made me a green sash, and I carried a wooden anchor on a green pillow. When I asked why the anchor, she said the anchor was a symbol, and it was supposed to give us hope for the future, but she was not very specific what we were to hope for. I wondered what kind of future she had in mind—my private future, like salvation of my soul or Father coming home; or some public future, like the demise of German revisionists, or victory over American imperialists, or maybe still something else.

The only relief from boredom during the school marching sessions was our principal, Mr. Zalewski himself. He was a tall, gaunt man on whom suits hung and flapped loosely like rags on a scarecrow would. His back was stiff, and when he wanted to look back, it was his whole body that he turned around, not just his head.

He loved parades, marches, and assemblies, and during our practice in the schoolyard, he shuffled along our column, rhythmically blowing his whistle to induce more spirit and enthusiasm into our sagging bodies. Because of this, and also on the account of his small, square mustache, he was called "Mein Führer" behind his back. Holding an eraser between my teeth in place of a whistle, I was trying to imitate the way Mein Führer walked, his flailing arms, long legs, sort of loose in the joints and attached to a rigid body. Maggie giggled, and Mein Führer spun his rigid body around faster than I had anticipated.

"Kooorsak! On the bench in front of my office! Waiting!"

I spent the rest of the afternoon sitting on the wooden bench next to Mein Führer's office, swinging my legs, watching flies crawling on the ceiling, spitting at the ones crawling on the floor, and generally being bored out of my mind. This was part of my punishment. The next part was the note addressed to Mama. Mein Führer handed me the note when he finally showed up long after everyone had gone home and the school hallways and classrooms became all quiet.

I walked home very slowly. My book bag with the note in it was heavier than usual. The sun had already fallen behind the church steeples and tall buildings on the other bank of the river. I stopped by the window in the stairwell to see the fiery sky and the dark silhouettes of trees sharply outlined against it. The air was still, and the whole world seemed to have come to a standstill too. Again I thought about the note resting in my backpack. Mein Führer wanted to speak to Mama about the problems I was having with "respect for authority." I thought what a rotten kid I turned out to be and how I always failed to consider Mama's feelings. She said often enough that I was just like my father, which must be true because I kept hurting her the way he did, and just like him, I would surely end up in the state slammer. That was when I heard someone crying. Short, little sobs and small whimpers. It was coming from our apartment. I was sure it was Mama, and I rushed in to beg her forgiveness and promise never again to imitate "Mein Führer." The door to our apartment was open, but I stopped in the hallway because I saw Mrs. W. sitting at our table in the big room, holding to her mouth with a trembling hand one of father's large plaid hankies. Her shoulders quivered. Mama sat across from her, holding her hand and patting it gently.

"I've no idea…" Mrs. W. was saying between sobs. "He could've gone…anywhere…jumped off the bridge…or something. He's not right in the head."

"Calm down, Brigida, dear, calm down. Take a sip of tea… It will do you good." Mama moved the sugar bowl closer to Mrs. W. "I'm sure he's quite all right in the head. Let's see…maybe we can figure this out… What did he say, exactly?"

Mrs. W. blew her nose.

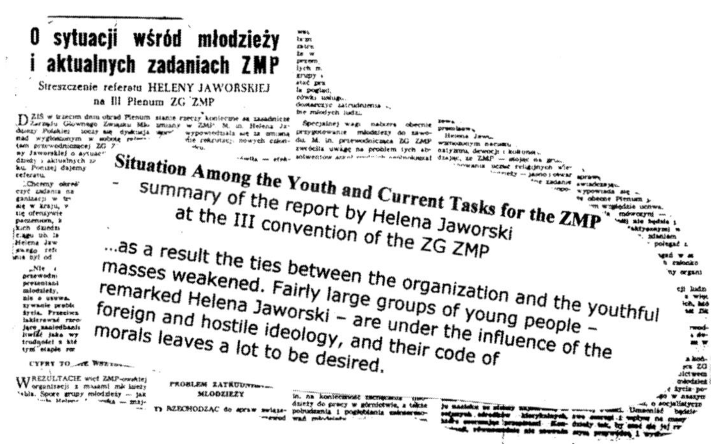

"He shook his fists at me and yelled, 'I'm gonna crush that louse who tattled…that worthless snitch…liar…' After that he didn't make any sense. Something about being kicked out of that

Socialistic Youth of his, about him being an agent of imperialism or something, some hidden map of America… You know darn well, Janie, I don't rightly understand any of this stuff. That boy is beyond me."

I was standing there in the hallway, in semi-darkness, listening to Mrs. W. and Mama when my elbows began to itch. I tried scratching them through the sleeves of the school uniform, but my backpack slid off my arm and crashed on the floor.

"It must be Agnes," Mama said. "Come in here, Aggie. Maybe you can help us figure it out." I would have much rather stayed out of it, not knowing what had happened. I had a feeling that, whatever it was, the map of America figured prominently in it.

The map of America—I was absolutely and recklessly in love with the idea and very proud it was mine. Knowing that the map was really nothing other than the mix of most revolting things one can think of, like sewage, mold and fungi of all sorts, seeping from the old, fractured underground pipes, I thought it was exceedingly clever of me to have connected the shape of the disgusting stain on the wall with the map of the rotten, capitalist state known for "keeping its working masses hungry, poor, and in appalling living conditions." No one I knew at the time owned and kept at home any large maps of the world or foreign countries. For someone to own a wall-size map of America hidden behind blankets was very suspect indeed. I shared the news of the map's discovery with only my closest friends who also thought it was remarkable for me to uncover secretly hidden "rotten map of a rotten state," but during the next few days the news had spread and by now every other kid in my class knew about it. Some had even visited the site and swore they saw it there, as clearly as I did. A few met Roman and were chased away by him, which only further enhanced the attraction. Thanks to the map, the forbidden territory where it was hidden, and the circumstances of my rescue, I attained a limited celebrity status and was thoroughly enjoying it while it lasted.

But there was something sinister in the parts of conversation between Mama and Mrs. W. Something that made me think I was the louse, the snitch, and the liar in question and that payback time was near. And there were those wretched goose bumps and my elbows itching and itching again.

Mama knew that the idea of the map was mine and that it was somehow connected to whatever had happened to Roman and his career in the Socialist Youth movement. I stood by the door to our big room, mortified she was going to give me away to Mrs. W. Instead, she did what made me momentarily believe in the ultimate justice, and timely, equitable punishment for sins, even the ones the catechism did not specifically mention. They were nameless sins, such as could only be identified by a feeling of wrongdoing and responsibility, which comes from our inside. Sins that could not be confessed or forgiven.

Mama said, "I'm going to make some more tea for Brigida and myself. You, Aggie, run over to her place and see if, by some chance, Roman is back. If so, bring him back here with you." This simply amounted to a death sentence.

I had circled the block in agony several times before approaching the ruins of the building where Mrs. W. and Roman lived. The streets were already dark, and the light in their low window was visible once you were close enough to the site. It really didn't mean that anyone was there because they often kept the lamps on in an effort to dry the surface of the wall. Standing at the top of the staircase leading to the cellar, I was still hoping Roman would not be there. Then it would be simple. I'd go home and truthfully report that he was still gone. If I went home without checking and told them he was not there while he, indeed, was already back home, the truth would come out sooner or later, and there would be questions about why I did what I did. The remaining alternative was unimaginable. For a long while I just stood there, scratching my elbows and listening.

I made my way down slowly. Quietly. One step at the time. At the foot of the staircase, I was feeling my way in the dark when the door was flung open and Roman appeared. The light from the room was behind him, and I could not see his face but his silhouette seemed menacingly large. There was no time or place to hide. I was in full view, at the bottom of the steps, in front of his door. He grabbed the lapels of my coat, picked me up, turned around, and pinned me to the wall by the door. I hung like a helpless puppet on a hook, feet dangling at least half a meter off the ground, while he kept me at arm's length, examining me like a pinned bug in a biology lab with disgust yet a certain degree of curiosity. I knew he was deciding how I was to die!

Suddenly with the light on his face, I saw that he was crying. Roman crying! A boy and almost grown up—crying! But there it was. He was biting his lips in an effort to stop the tears, but his eyes were red and wet, and his chin still quivering. Although pinned to the wall, I felt greatly relieved. The fact that he was crying had somehow saved me. He was spent, and all the hate had drained out of him. My presence was simply an exasperating nuisance. He let go of my coat unexpectedly, and I slid along the wall to the ground. One contemptuous glance in my direction and shaking his head, he said quietly more to himself than to me, "Bourgeois bastard." Then he pulled his jacket about him and was off climbing the stairs, two steps at the time, not looking back at me or the open door he had left behind. The sound of his steps died down, and I was still lying there, leaning against the wall, a rumpled heap unable to move. Next to me in the shaft of light from the door, I recognized the dirty rag upon which I had tripped on my first visit here.

Landscapes

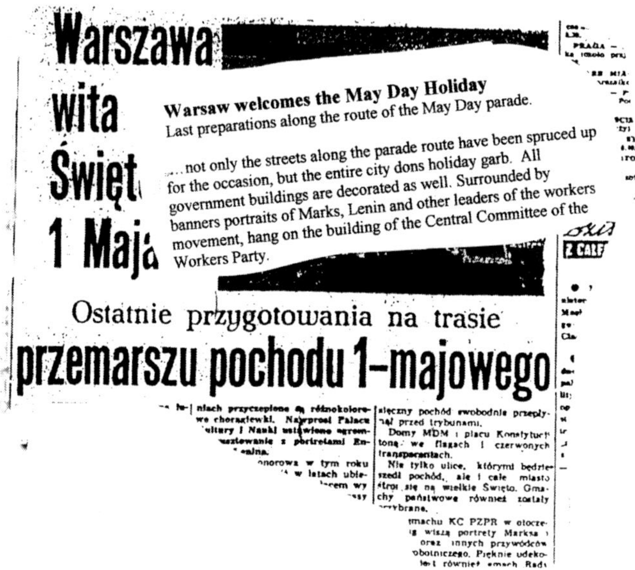

As I look back at the places I grew up in, at the changing seasons, and at our life there, I sometimes think of our life as a motif in a painting of a landscape. Life as a thread of carmine winding through dry, leafless bushes, rendered in washed-out browns, and through white trunks of birches shedding yellow feathers. A flash of intensity.

I think of clouds somber and gray, hanging over buildings, ruptured stucco revealing red wounds of raw brick, bleeding against the backdrop of wet, slick, charcoal rooftops. Beneath, pearl mist wrapping the black trunks of bare oaks.

I think of it as a young beech in late autumn, suddenly erupting in scarlet flames among the golden glow of maples or larches interlaced with juicy green pines, and burning in the cold, piercing blue air.

Or of the landscape of vast white stillness where to the side, at the line of horizon, the crimson sun is slowly dying, sinking into cool purples—there runs a thin line the color of blood. Drawn with one stroke. Ending abruptly. Life as a motif in a landscape.

On the morning of May first, Mein Führer expected all of us to turn out in school uniforms topped off with red scarves given out by Mrs. Pawlak. On that day I really should have been there, marching with my class in the May Day Parade, but instead Mama, Aunt Rita, Uncle Henry, Fishel, and I, we were all driving out into the country. I was already preparing a small bundle of lies, which I would tell Mein Führer next day at school. I had no qualms about lying. Everybody lies.

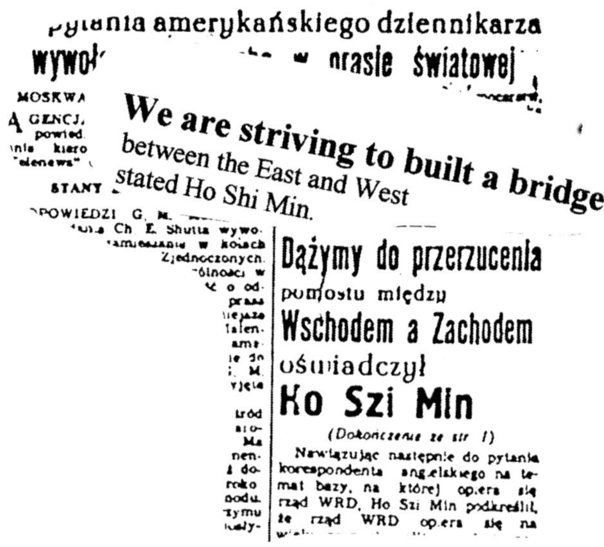

Mama said they lie on the radio and on the newsreels shown before the movies. Fishel said the movies are a stack of lies too. According to all Father's friends, the news in the papers was "doctored to communist advantage," which I thought meant untrue. And then Father and Uncle Bert must have also been lying about what they did in the co-op 134 before they got arrested. True, in the very beginning I saw some buttons in different colors and sizes, but later, whenever Father brought me there the machines at the co-op were unplugged, cold, and covered with a thick layer of dust. Dr. Landau also lied when he gave Mama phony certificates saying that Father was sick so that she could try to get him out of prison before his time. Because of these lies, he was allowed to receive packages with more food. Before last Easter I even saw Father Simon through the crack in the curtain, sitting in the confessional, picking his nose and rolling the boogers between his fingers while he was supposed to be praying for Mama's absolution. She didn't see it because she bowed her head, and later she received Holy Communion without even knowing she still had all her sins. Truth and lies seemed to be all mixed up; it was impossible to tell them apart. It depended on who said it, when they said it, and who listened. You had to be very careful.

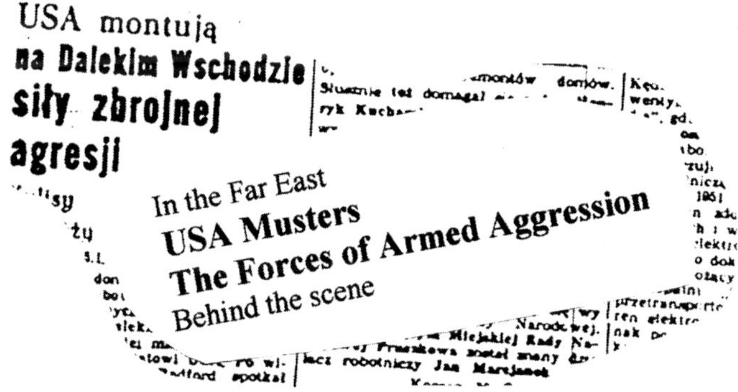

Mr. Zalewski was undoubtedly going to question me and others who also ditched the proletarian holiday and perhaps he would even write another note to Mama. But I wouldn't have missed this trip for anything. Rarely did I get to go for a picnic and ride in the shiny, new car at the same time. This one belonged to Uncle Henry. He was driving, and Rita, his wife, was sitting up front, next to him. I had a window seat in the back, next to Mama, who was between Fishel and me. We were a bit crowded on the back seat because we also had Mama's orange blanket and the baskets filled with food and lemonade, for me, and *something stronger* for the grown-ups. Fishel put his arm around Mama and tickled me on the back of my neck. I knew he was being playful, but I got impatient with him. This ride was so special! The wind from the open window whistled songs of longing straight into my ears, and sights unfolded at every turn of the road; I'd rather be left alone. I wanted to take it all in so that it became a part of me, and would be mine, forever.

We came to the crest of the hill, and a valley opened up to the empty sky. A patchwork of fields covered its floor. The furrows wove purposeful, intricate patterns. Over some there already hung a green breath of new growth. Others were still dark, moist, expectant. In the heart of the valley, the wide stretch of sloping meadow met the sluggish river. Here we turned off the main road. Uncle Henry slowed down, and the car gently bounced on the soft dirt road. The grasses grew higher and higher the closer we got to the river. The air was vibrating with the thin buzzing songs of flies and the deeper murmur of hornets, wasps, and bumblebees. The tall grasses were poking their long heads through the open windows of the car.

Next to the river there was a small area where the grass was cleared. We carried our blankets and baskets. Uncle Henry took a bottle of vodka from the trunk. He had four glasses wrapped in a towel. The grass was up to my hips. It fell away under the heavy thread of Uncle Henry's boots when I followed him.

A row of silver poplars lined the bank of the shallow river. I wished I could just drop everything right there, kick off my shoes, and get my feet wet—but I knew better. I had to be good and really helpful so that when I finally asked to go into the water, Mama wouldn't be able to refuse. Aunt Rita was very particular about every little thing. She even brought her linen tablecloth, which was now being spread upon the top of the blanket, on the grass. Between Mama and Aunt Rita, they had enough food for at least a week. Cold chicken, hard-boiled eggs, pickles, sausage—this was going to be a very long lunch. Resigned to the fact that the river would have to wait for a little while longer, I started picking at a chicken drumstick.

The sun felt so good on my back that if it weren't for the river winking at me from beyond the gray poplar leaves, I would have fallen asleep. Uncle Henry was certainly ready to do so. "Come," he said to Aunt Rita, "put your old man to sleep." I could tell he'd had more than enough vodka. He knocked over an empty bottle as he got up. He took Aunt Rita by the neck, and they both trudged through the grass toward the car. Mama and Fishel sat side by side on the other end of the blanket. Their faces were also flushed, partly from the vodka and partly from the sun. I thought this was a good time to introduce the idea of getting my toes wet. It went over surprisingly well. "Leave your shoes here, Aggie," Mama said, "so you don't have to worry about the current taking them away."

When I finally turned away from the river and looked around, I was struck by the openness, the vastness of the place—the curve of the hill against the sky and the rich green furrows cutting into its side. The blue top of the car floated above the grass, somehow unmoored from its wheels, rocking gently. My heart went still, and then I started running in panic, thinking they might have been looking for me and now were leaving without me. But as I got closer, the car stopped moving. There seemed to be no one inside it. Now I was embarrassed for having panicked like a child.

I pulled a long blade of grass; I bit on its end and casually ambled toward the car as if nothing had happened. I came to a stop when I saw a tangle of human legs through the open window. I realized they belonged to Aunt Rita and Uncle Henry. I also realized that they were lying side by side on the unfolded seats, and both had no underwear. Uncle Henry was very hairy. His entire legs and bottom were covered with thick black fuzz. One of his legs was up, resting on Aunt Rita's pink hip. There was also a strange wrinkled piece of skin resting on Uncle Henry's thigh. It didn't look like a part of his body but something that belonged to someone else, dropped there accidentally and forgotten. My throat was very dry, and I couldn't take my eyes off their exposed private parts. After watching them for a while, I realized that they were both somehow connected at the crotch. Then, slowly, Aunt Rita shifted and a small, shiny, silver fish slid out from the fold between her legs. It lay completely still, as if dead, on Uncle Henry's hairy thigh. I intuitively knew I should not have been looking, that it was a sin to look and to do what they were doing. I did not want anyone to see me looking, yet the sight of their exposed bodies had an irresistible pull. I was torn between leaving and looking just a little longer….

"Where are you, Aggie? Answer me," I heard Mama's voice. It was coming from the river.

I quietly knelt and sat on my heels by the blanket. Now that I was in her sight, Mama did not seem interested in what happened at the riverbank or in Uncle Henry's car. I was relieved she didn't question me. Fishel lay stretched out on his back, taking up most of the blanket. His head was cradled in the palms of his hands. Mama sat beside him, her knees drawn up to her chest.

"Theo told me you're Jewish," she said, "but he never said you were a country boy." Her voice broke the silence filled only with the buzzing of the meadow.

Fishel's head turned abruptly. "Does it make a difference?" he asked. The sun was in his eyes, and he squinted, which made him look angry.

Mama leaned over him with such tender eagerness that I became instinctively alarmed. There was a subtle undercurrent, something intangible, a flimsy, invisible thread connecting Mama and Fishel in a special way that excluded me. It made me very uneasy.

My foot had gone to sleep, and I had ants in my toes. I massaged my foot while watching them from under my falling hair. "Don't be silly," Mama said, "of course not. It's just that Theo once said you come from Lublin, so I naturally assumed it was your hometown."

"My folks were from the area of Vilnus. In Lublin I had an uncle, David Stain. He also had a large family, all lost in Auschwitz. Rounded up by Gestapo in 1942," said Fishel. His eyes followed a hawk that fell from the sky into the tall grasses by the river. Moments later it rose heavily, carrying its prey—a small, gray rabbit.

"Where were you in 1942?" asked Mama.

"I lived with them," Fishel said very softly. "It was just a coincidence. They had a bakery in a Jewish section of town. On the day they were all put on the transport train to Auschwitz, I was picking up three sacks of flower from a farm outside of Lublin." The hawk disappeared among the poplars. Fishel followed with his eyes its slow descent and then added, "It was the second time I cheated fate. After the war, in 1949, out of guilt I went back to Lublin, to Red Cross, to register the missing family. I made them search old German transport lists. Not all my cousins were on those lists. My youngest niece, Mirah, was not there—I mean, her name was not on the list. The Red Cross woman said that sometimes those who were shot during the loading, at the station, were not entered on the lists. Mirah was only ten years old… They said they will search, but there's not much hope."

I thought I knew what Fishel meant when he talked about guilt. I was twelve, and I was alive.

"You're so young and already have such a past…" Mama said. "…but when you're young, it doesn't matter as much," she added after a moment of thoughtful silence.

"But it does," said Fishel. "The past is a hump, a living part of us. It's with us wherever we go. It does matter. The truth is we don't have a choice. Our past places on us indistinct but numerous restrictions. In this way it predetermines our future. Look at yourself and this child." He motioned with his head toward me.

Mama looked at the ground instead, and with the point of her shoe, drew a deep ravine across the path of the army of tiny, black ants marching toward the river.

"Let's talk about you," she said, throwing her head backwards. "I want to know what you did as a boy. Did you steal apples? Or maybe tied burning papers to cats' tails? Where are your folks? Why did you leave them?"

I looked at Fishel. I was trying to imagine him barefoot and in short pants. It was a useless exercise because no matter how I changed his body, his face remained the same. Gentle, yet dark and melancholy, a grown-up face attached to the body of a child or a teenager.

Fishel turned on his side and raised himself on his elbow. His face was now very close to Mama's. A strand of her long black hair was blown across his cheek by the breeze. "I left them in late August," he said, "in 1941."

This sounded like the beginning of a story. Fishel told good, gory stories. They always ended with someone dying. I remembered a lot of them from our winter sessions at the Co-op

No.134, before Father and Uncle Bert got arrested. They were playing cards then, as if nothing was going to happen. Or maybe they played because they somehow knew, or felt, it was going to happen, and they were just killing time waiting for it. Anyway, Fishel's stories had a slow, rocking music in them. His voice came in small waves, tirelessly caressing the ear, whispering, humming the song of Fishel…

"In late August, 1941, a unit of the German Army swept through our village," Fishel said slowly, as if hesitating…

His village was a small, peaceful place, off the main road, between the town of Kaunas and Vilnius, where the Niemen River was wide and slow. He was then fifteen. Germans were sent to round up men and boys to widen the main road for the advancing Wehrmacht. But the news of the brutality, hunger, and death that came with the German Army reached the village first and sent all the men and boys into the woods long before the soldiers arrived. He went into the woods too with his father and two brothers. But he couldn't stay there long. He grew restless as he listened to the distant roar of truck engines. He'd always had this inexplicable longing for the machines. He'd seen them several times on trips with his father to the market in Vilnius. His father said they were called automobiles and could move by themselves and carry people and sometimes cargo too. A few times he'd even managed to speak to the drivers who waited for their masters leaning against the slick, black machines parked in front of important looking buildings. By the time the Germans came to his village, he knew what made the automobiles go, what made them stop. He knew there was an engine, the magical source of power that made them move. So when he heard those engines roar in the late summer air, he grew restless and left the woods. But at fifteen, he was no fool. He had a keen sense of danger. Just as he knew when and where to cross the slow river on foot, he knew when and where to approach the Germans to get a glimpse, maybe even touch their machines.

The only brick building in the village was really beyond it, where the cobblestone road through the village ended and the sandy dirt deposited over the centuries by the flooding river began. Everyone called the empty structure *the armory*, but no one remembered why. His father said that it probably went back to the time of Tsar Nicholas and the great Bolshevik Revolution. Now the Germans set up camp in and around the armory. Their automobiles, machines big and small, were all around the building. He hovered around there unseen, fascinated, longing to get close enough to touch. The machines were different than the ones he had seen in the city. These had no roofs, and their sides were partially opened too. But they were machines all the same. So he lingered close, peering down through the leaves of the oaks and then flat in the tall summer grass and in the ditch by the roadside. A shadow among shadows.

When the soldiers swept through the village at dawn, they rounded up only eleven men—fools who either thought they could hide on their farms and outwit the Germans or those who could not keep their longing for a woman in check and came back from the woods in the night just for a few hours. By nightfall, all eleven were locked up in the armory basement whose old door was now reinforced with fresh pine beams. But this did not concern him.

He sensed danger, so he laid low in the grass, chewing on a hardened piece of cheese. He felt that luck was with him. Earlier a soldier had come to one of the machines and climbed in. He had cleaned the seats and the floor and then started the engine. The soldier's every move was etched in his memory. Then the soldier jumped out and lifted one side of the hood. He leaned over the humming engine then closed the hood and pulled the keys. He slipped them into a pocket from which a large, gray rag was hanging. He bent to check the wheels, front and back, and then went around the machine. There he pulled the rag from his pocket. Out with it came the keys silently falling into the dry, sandy dirt. The soldier used the rag to wipe the glass window and the lights up front. Then he stuffed the rag back in his pocket and went back into the building.

Fishel trembled with excitement and finally had to bite his lip to steady himself. Silently he waited until darkness embraced the buildings, the people, and the machines. The guard was posted, and his cigarette glowed in the dark like a little bright star. He waited until the night grew dense, and the cigarette died in the dirt under the soldier's foot. Now he became a snake in the grass, curving and gliding noiselessly forward, forward, forward. There were three keys on the thick metal chain. He fingered them gently and learned their shapes by heart. And then he became the snake again and curved his body along the wheel and up the step and smoothly slipped inside the machine. His hands lovingly held the wheel and caressed the gages and levers. His finger felt the opening for the key. He tried the first one, and it jammed. Patiently, slowly he worked to remove it. He tried the next, and it slid effortlessly into place. It belonged.

He stopped and looked at the sky. His heart was pounding so hard that he was sure even God, wherever he was, could hear it. The moon was creeping up the roof of the armory. Once it looked over the top, the machines would be all aglow in its cool, silver light. Now that he possessed the machine, he had to have a plan before the treacherous moon, perched on the rooftop, would give him away.

Turn the wheel left, and after about ten meters hit the cobble stones, then push the right and middle levers to the floor, and go straight on the cobblestone road through the village to the bridge, then on the bridge, push the left and middle lever to the floor, and turn off the key; then jump in the water and swim with the current to the sandbar downstream, which was thickly overgrown with reeds—this was his plan. He closed his eyes and in his memory repeated the exact movements of the soldier when he started the machine, drove it, and stopped it. He ran through the sequence in his mind one more time, locating in the dark the stick, on which his right hand was supposed to rest, and all three levers on the floor. Now he was ready.

The roar of the engine filled the night. Like a cry of a wounded animal, it tore the dark silence to shreds. He was on the cobblestones and pushed the lever with his right foot all the way to the floor. The engine whined and begged he didn't know for what. Shots rang out behind him, but he was not concerned. He was swallowing the wind and thought his breast would burst from it.

The bridge was narrow. Only one horse cart at the time could pass above the river. In the dark, the right side of the machine hit a wooden pole, and he was thrown from the seat. When he came to, steam was rising from the machine, and he could hear the other engines roaring. He took one last, longing look at the machine and then slid silently into the river. He swam with the current for a good half an hour without looking back. He dragged himself ashore through the tall reeds and over the carpet of water lilies. When he reached the trees, he sat down and rested until the cool night air made him shiver. He wrung the water from his clothes and put them back on, looked upon the river, basking in the moonlight, then turned and walked into the darkness of the woods.

His progress was slow. In the woods the night was as thick as beet borscht, and he was unable to find and follow a path. Instead he followed the moon, which sporadically appeared and disappeared through the tangled branches of the dark and distant treetops. He tried to estimate his position relative to the moon, the passing time, and the village. He wanted to go home. At dawn, when the woods became silver, he came across four men. He thought they were from the Resistance because one had a small gun wedged behind his wide belt. They were not from his village but knew the woods well and pointed him home. They also gave him some cooked venison and a stale biscuit and then dissolved into the graying trees. When he reached the village in mid-morning, he fell into the grass again.

Around the armory the remaining old men, women, and children were gathered. Soldiers stood around them with rifles. The people had stone faces; only a few children cried, hanging on to their mothers' skirts. Wladyslaw, the tall, wiry blacksmith was standing against the back wall of the armory. Lying snake-like, low in the grass, he heard the shots but could not see where they came from. He just saw Wladyslaw's knees fold, as if in prayer, and then the man disappeared behind the wall of tall grass.

That afternoon the German unit left the village, towing behind them the machine with a crushed front end. After their departure, the village men came home from the woods. During that time the boy grew even more restless. The connection, he felt existed, between the "sabotaged" machine and the folding of Wladyslaw's knees became oppressive. It replayed itself in his mind over and over again in detail: the shots, the knees, and the tall grass.

One night when he woke up after dreaming of the knees again, he took a loaf of bread and some cheese and left his house for the woods. He walked slowly south. Toward the end of the day, he saw the city of Vilnius from the distance. That night when he sat on the soft moss in the woods and chewed the crust of the bread and the cheese, he decided to go into the city the following morning and find a church.

He started before dawn. When the sky in the east became transparent and the soft, white glow rose above the horizon, he found a church. He looked it over carefully. He had never been inside of one. Father took him into the synagogue a few times while they were in Vilnius on the market days, but the church he knew nothing about. Yet he felt he had to go since Wladyslaw had been a man who went to church, not to a synagogue. He went in when it was still gray outside. A small, red light was glowing on the platform raised against the opposite wall. He sat down in the darkest corner and wondered what to do next. As time passed, a few old women wrapped in black kerchiefs filed in, one by one. Their faces were parched, and wrinkled, and made out of dust.

The light was first silver, then white, and then at sunrise it boldly danced in through the multi-colored glass. It threw colors on the gray stone floor, and it illuminated the dust that filled the air. He had come here to redeem himself. He wanted his knees to fold just like Wladyslaw's, in prayer. But the place was full of the dancing dust—dust that might have come off the faces of the dried up women, wrapped in black. Leaving, he held his breath in order not to take in the dust. He carried his burden of bread and cheese farther and farther south. Around him the knees of many men were folding; some in prayer, but most in death.

The silence was lazy in the afternoon sun, which hung low over the hill. I was sitting quietly, trying to put Fishel back together. After his story, the Fishel I knew came apart at the seams. Until now he made sense to me. I used to know him as someone who told good and bloody stories, brought chickens when there were none to be had in the state meat stores, freed my head from the bars of Mrs. Wyglondalo's window, and made Mama shriek with laughter. Now I had quite a different Fishel to deal with: a boy, barely older than myself, stealing German cars, hiding in the woods, watching death, and finally setting out on his own upon a strange journey with no destination. I also felt that the boy was somehow implicated in the death of the man from the story. Fishel's slim, dark body looked to me pretty much as before, although it was now inhabited by two distinct persons: Boy Fishel and Fishel I Know.

"Don't be so sad, princess," Mama said, stroking my cheek. She was letting me know how she felt and that she expected me to feel it as well.

The Route of the May Day March will run along the Aleje Jerozolimske towards the Poniatowski Bridge.

The working masses of the capital, farmers from the Warsaw Region, as well as the youth and various sports groups will all participate in the May Day Parade

The construction crew of the Josef Stalin's Palace of Culture and Science will also take part in the festivities.

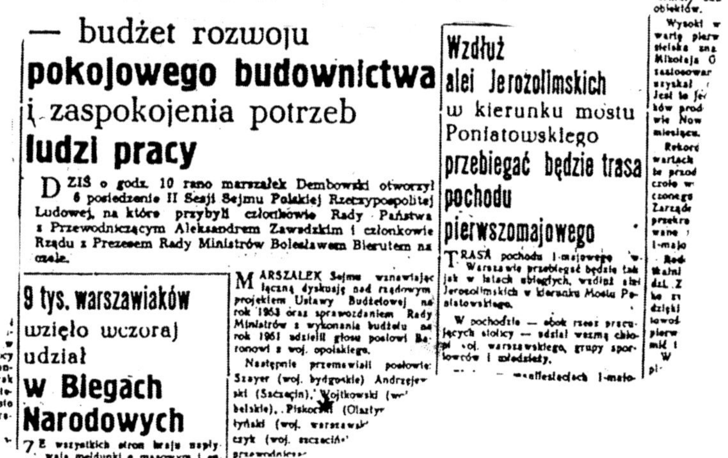

— budżet rozwoju
pokojowego budownictwa
i zaspokojenia potrzeb
ludzi pracy

DZIŚ o godz. 10 rano marszałek Dembowski otworzył 6 posiedzenie II Sesji Sejmu Polskiej Rzeczypospolitej Ludowej, na które przybyli członkowie Rady Państwa z Przewodniczącym Aleksandrem Zawadzkim i członkowie Rządu z Prezesem Rady Ministrów Bolesławem Bierutem na czele.

9 tys. warszawiaków
wzięło wczoraj
udział
w Biegach Narodowych

Z wszystkich stron kraju napływają meldunki o masowym i … udziale w Biegach Na…

MARSZAŁEK Sejmu wznawiając łączną dyskusję nad rządowym projektem Ustawy Budżetowej na rok 1953 oraz sprawozdaniem Rady Ministrów z wykonania budżetu na rok 1951 udzielił głosu posłowi Baronowi z woj. opolskiego.

Następnie przemawiali posłowie: Szayer (woj. bydgoskie) Andrzejewski (Szczecin), Wojtkowski (w… belskie), Piskorski (Olsztyn…) …tyński (woj. warszaw… …czyk (woj. szczeciń… …przewodnicz…

Wzdłuż alei Jerozolimskich w kierunku mostu Poniatowskiego przebiegać będzie trasa pochodu pierwszomajowego

TRASA pochodu 1-majowego w Warszawie przebiegać będzie tak jak w latach ubiegłych, wzdłuż alei Jerozolimskich w kierunku Mostu Poniatowskiego.

W pochodzie — obok rzesz pracujących stolicy — udział wezmą chłopi woj. warszawskiego, grupy sportowców i młodzieży.

The sun slipped behind the hill, whose dark edge was outlined against the fiery sky. By the river the silver poplars were really saffron yellow. Their long shadows stretched across the river like ghost bridges. Where we were the deep blue shadow had settled. From a distant hill, on the other side of the valley, we were indiscernible, car and all, except perhaps for Mama's bright orange blanket. In the shade, Mama's face looked pale and drawn in. She struggled to get up from the ground as if a terrible burden was placed upon her. "Oh, my back!" she moaned, and Fishel clumsily tried to help her up. He didn't see that besides his life story, she was already struggling under the weight of my father's story and her own and the life stories of all the others for whom she had ever felt love or compassion.

Chinese Porcelain

At the end of June, a summer storm lingered at the edge of the river and over the city on the other side. Time and again the lightning touched the surface of the water and then retreated back into the clouds. The air was still and full of all kinds of flies, mosquitoes, and other bugs. Mama said that's how it always was before a storm. Birds were crazy too, flying low and making loud, shrill noises. I guess they were happy because of the bugs. Mama was all sweaty, and her cheeks were flushed. She rushed back and forth, putting away all the newspapers displayed outside the stand. The rain could start at any moment.

"Hurry up, Aggie. Hand me those packets of the *Express Wieczorny* and *Trybuna*." she said. "I wonder where Fishel is; he promised to help in case of rain. Well, the rain is almost here, but he isn't."

It had been two months since Mama started running the newspaper stand on the corner of Obroncow and Francuska streets, next to the pharmacy. She had also taken to bringing home the papers she sold every day. She was usually too tired to read them, but I started looking them over from time to time. Most of the stuff was boring, but sometimes I found things that were interesting. Mama was still very nervous about running the stand and also very impatient. I had to watch my step; otherwise she would whack me across my back. Sometimes I didn't even know why.

It all started back in April, about the time my head got stuck in Mrs. Wyglondalo's window. Uncle Henry came by one night while Fishel and Mama were having tea in the kitchen. I was in Mama's room, at the big table, copying designs from the Chinese vase, which belonged to Grandma Aniela. Grandma Aniela was already dead, but she gave this vase to Father before she died. She gave Mama a red robe made of real silk. The robe was very precious. On the back it had a dragon embroidered with golden thread. Mama kept the robe in the wardrobe between two sheets of paper. She never wore it. The vase was usually wrapped in an old blanket and also stashed away in the wardrobe. Sometimes when Mama wanted to keep me busy, she would take the vase out and let me copy the pictures. I loved this vase. I wished it could be mine. I wished Father would give it to me before he died. It was the most beautiful thing I had ever seen. It was even prettier than the picture of the Madonna and the angel in the side nave of our church. The porcelain was so thin that you could see the light right through it. Once Fishel put a candle inside it, and the light made all the little people on the vase come alive. Two geishas with pink umbrellas were waiting for a rickshaw. They were on the tiny arched bridge. It was spring because all the trees had pink blossoms. The geishas were all dressed up in kimonos— green and blue. One of them was turning around to look at me. She had a golden dragon on the back of her kimono. The sun was rising. It was big and round like a peach.

The day Uncle Henry came, I was trying to copy the geisha with the golden dragon in my notebook. Mama made me move to the corner of the table because she wanted to serve tea to Uncle Henry too, and there was not enough room in the kitchen for both Fishel and Uncle Henry. Uncle Henry said that Mr. Krentz, who ran the newspaper stand, died of a heart attack and that Mrs. Krentz was too old to run the stand by herself.

"Imagine, Janie, if Mrs. Krentz kept her license and hired you to run the stand—" he was saying when Mama interrupted.

"But I don't know anything about running a newspaper stand. Why would Mrs. Krentz hire someone who can't do what they are hired to do?"

"What's there to know about stacking and selling papers? At first she would just have to show you the ropes," said Uncle Henry.

"Would she be willing to do that?" asked Mama.

"She wants to sell the license, take the money, and move to the country to live with her sister. But who has the kind of money it would take to buy her out?" Uncle Henry explained. "If she wants to move, she'll have to settle for less. You run the stand for her and send her some money, let's say even half of the money, every month. No, no, half is too much. Maybe she'll agree to less than that…"

We got up very early. When it was still dark. Mama made oatmeal and then left to receive the daily delivery. The streetlights were still on, but the sky in the east was beginning to turn violet and pink. Through the kitchen window, I watched Mama go until she turned the corner into Obroncow Street. She always waved to me before she disappeared.

Kioskarze nie otrzymują tego co zamawiają w „Ruchu"

a ich klienci też mają powód do narzekań

gdy nie mogą zaprenumerować gazety i wodę „Poemat" muszą kupować na

PROSZĘ o papier listowy — mówi klient pochylony kiem ulicznego kiosku „Ruchu".
— Nie mam — odpowiada sprzedawca — ale mam za to

Kiosk Operators Do Not Receive the Merchandise They Had Ordered. Their customers also have reasons to complain: they are unable to buy newspaper subscriptions and cologne "Poem" is available only in half-a-liter bottles.

Often Fishel came to help her with the papers in the morning and sometimes during the day too. There he was now crossing the street, heading our way. He was running because first drops of rain were beginning to fall. They were very big. They made splatters on the pavement at least as wide as half of my hand. When such big drops fell down with gravity and all that, they must have weighed a ton. I wondered if a drop like that falling down could knock a bird right out of the sky if it happened to hit it on the head.

"Agnes, didn't I ask you to cover those stacks with the tarpaulin? And there you are with your head up watching the rain fall!" Mama was mad, but Fishel was already here to rescue me.

"I'll help her with that," he said. "The tarpaulin is too big for her to handle."

Against the wall of the stand, packets of *Pravda* were stacked five high. Fishel leaned over the papers, pulling the tarpaulin.

"*Pravda*…the Russian-language version? Why the hell are you getting so many of these? Who buys this shit, anyway?" he said. Mama looked nervously around. People were opening umbrellas or rushing out of the rain. There was already that "just-before-the rain" smell in the air.

"No one," Mama said, "and don't be so loud. We'll all end up in a slammer, just like Theo." She came over and helped us to tuck the tarpaulin around the papers. "The newsstands able to sell more than one hundred of these daily"—she continued— "get a bonus at the end of the month, so I made a deal with Mrs. Bronski…"

"Do I know Mrs. Bronski?" asked Fishel.

"She's the fat lady who sells veggies from a cart, two blocks down," I volunteered.

"…but Communist ideology is her real, secret passion," said Fishel.

Mama burst out laughing. "Oh, knock it off!" she said and playfully pushed Fishel against the newspapers. "Mrs. Bronski is always short of paper to wrap her carrots or potatoes. She takes *Pravda* off my hands at a discount, and we get fresh vegetables free and a cash bonus from the state."

"Look at you, Janie! And who would have thought! You are turning in to a true capitalist bloodsucker! I'm so proud..." Fishel grabbed Mama, lifted her up, and set her on the stack of newspapers.

She looked at me, and I knew she was embarrassed. She quickly jumped off the stack and put her arm around me.

"Why don't you get the keys, your book bag, and run home," she said. "Fishel will help me board up the front, and we'll be right over."

I wished she'd let me stay with them. I liked to see her when she was laughing and Fishel when he was kidding her like that, but I knew there was no use asking when she had her mind set on something. "Quick, quick," she said, "before it really starts coming down." I went inside the stand to get my books and keys while Fishel gathered today's papers displayed in the front.

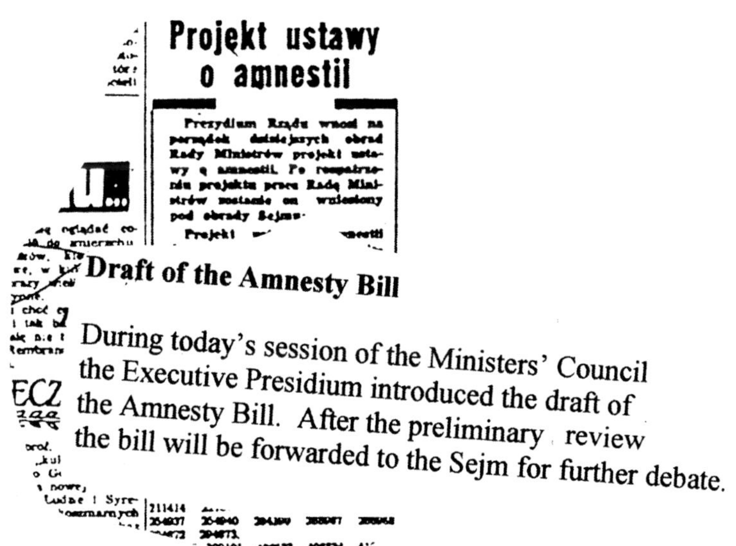

"Did you see this?" he called out to Mama, waving the paper and pointing to the first page. Mama never read the papers. She was always too busy stacking, displaying, and selling them. "Amnesty!" he cried. "They are announcing amnesty for the twenty-second of July, to celebrate the state holiday!"

A sudden gust of wind picked up some papers still left on the front display. It tossed them in the air, and they flapped their wings, flying low over the pavement, like giant black-and-white birds trying to stay airborne. I was surprised that neither Mama nor Fishel was going after them.

The door to our apartment was old and warped. The paint was coming off, especially right around the doorknob. To open it you had to pull hard and turn the key at the same time. I was fighting with the door when Mrs. Oggler appeared, coming down the stairs in her gray spring coat topped off with a silk scarf. She filled the width of the staircase. Mrs. Oggler was big. I mean, really big. She looked down on most people I knew and had an awful loud voice too. Her face got red when she talked, and her nose, which usually looked like strawberry, seemed to get even bigger and redder when she was mad. Her hair was tightly braided and pinned into a round bun on the top of her head. She was our upstairs neighbor and Mama's best friend.

I didn't like Mrs. Oggler much, but she was very good to Mama. Whenever Mama had a problem, or when she was just sad, she talked to Mrs. Oggler, and Mrs. Oggler said, "We girls got to stick together; otherwise men will make us dirt." I didn't know exactly who the men were and how they were going to do it. I'd been planning to ask Mama about it, but I had a feeling she would laugh.

Before the summer break, when I had homework and Mama had to be at the stand, Mrs. Oggler would feed me soup and sort of watch over me. Sometimes she even helped me with math. I didn't like her much, though, because she always asked me questions about Father, Mama, or Fishel, or even Uncle Henry and Aunt Rita. She wanted to know everything. Sometimes, while I did my assigned reading, she poked through our shelves in the kitchen, the wardrobe, and even under the bathroom sink where Mama stashed all sorts of junk behind the curtain made of an old sheet.

Mrs. Oggler had a white girl kitten. Her name was Snowy, and she was adorable. Snowy and I played a lot together, and when she was tired, she just curled up at my side and went to sleep, and her little motor hummed softly because she was happy. Everyone in our building knew Mrs. Oggler. She bought and sold meat and other stuff on the black market. She'd been doing it for years. Twice a week she brought the meat in large canvas bags from a village outside of Warsaw. She sold the meat to the people in our building and other buildings down the street. Because Mama and Mrs. Oggler were friends, she very often gave us a couple of pork chops or some country sausage. Mama always said that Mrs. Oggler took care of me, but it seemed that she was also taking care of Mama.

"So where's your mama? Selling papers in the rain?"

"She's coming, and Fishel too. They'll be here any minute."

"You want some help with that door? You in a hurry or something?"

"Yeah, sort of. I want to get to the dictionary. I need to look up a word."

"What's the word?"

"*Amnesty.*"

"*Amnesty?* Hmm…so where did you hear this word?" Mrs. Oggler's heavy paw rested on the doorknob, and the key immediately turned in the lock.

"Fishel saw it on the front page of the newspaper. It's going to happen on the twenty-second of July. I just want to know what it is."

"No need for you to go to the dictionary. Amnesty is when the state lets out a few small crooks from prison to make a good impression. Your father is a small crook, an amateur really. He might get out… Well, here's your mama and Fishel coming up. Look out the window, dearie, and tell me if the rain is heavy. I might have to get a taxi…"

I went to the window to look at the rain. *A crook! A small crook!* Mrs. Oggler's words were ringing in my head. She was the first person that called him by his real name. She named what he really was. No one else would. I knew he was devious, like a crook, because he lied about what he and his friends were doing, pretending to make buttons while they did entirely something else. What was it he did, I did not know. Probably something really awful because neither Mama nor Uncle Henry nor Fishel ever spoke a word about it. I was treated like small child by everyone who did not want to talk about him, I was lied to by him personally, and then I was deserted by him without an explanation. And all because I was too young to understand. Yes, I knew Mama prepared packages for him, and she wrote letters to prison authorities, telling them how sick he was, and how little money we had, but any time something important was discussed, she sent me out of the room. And just now it made me think that she knew all along what he was doing and quietly went along. And that made her somewhat guilty too. All this I thought about I had to keep to myself. Grandma T. had an old saying that Mama repeated many times when I had questions about things grownups did not want to talk about. She used to say, "Children and fish have no voice," and I knew I had to be quiet.

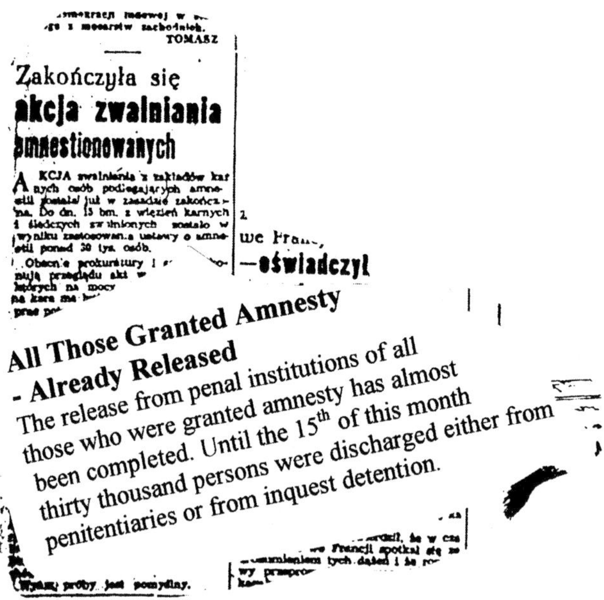

The light was best in our kitchen early in the morning. The window faced east, and I could see the sky. Small clouds were frosted pink at the edges, and they were floating in the air, which at this hour and for a very short time was turquoise, not blue like it usually was. That was why I liked to look at it at this time. Mama had turned the corner, and I could go back to copying in my special notebook another picture from the Chinese vase. Today I was doing the geisha in a turquoise kimono. She was holding a flowering branch. Fishel told me these pink flowers were cherry blossoms. I had no pink coloring pencil.

There was no school today, but Mama had a delivery of papers, and she had to keep the stand open until noon. Today was the state holiday—July 22nd. Before Mama left, she took out the Chinese vase to keep me busy and quiet. My father was sleeping in the big room. Mama went to get him yesterday afternoon.

Since the day we found out about the amnesty until the day she left to pick him up, Mama and I hadn't talked about Father at all. She must have assumed I somehow figured out he was coming back. On the other hand, after Mrs. Oggler called him *a small crook* that day in the stairwell, and after I realized that Mama was in on his secret all along, I did not feel like talking to her about him either. Since they took him away in December, we busied ourselves with everyday stuff, and he never was much talked about anyway, unless a food package needed to be sent or another petition written. But these last few weeks before his release, Mama became even quieter, and when we sometimes started talking about school, dinner, or what happened at the newsstand, after a few minutes her mind seemed to wander away, and our talk was soon going no where. When she went to get him, I waited at Mrs. Oggler's, playing with Snowy, but it got very late, and Mrs. Oggler sent me to bed. When I woke up in the middle of the night, Mama was sleeping at the edge of my bed, curled up under a blanket. Then I heard snoring from the big room.

I was trying to color the cherry blossoms pink by first using red, very lightly, and then white over the red. I wondered how it would be when he woke up. He probably forgot I had a birthday in May. He didn't know I was already twelve. He never remembered things like that. He used to ask a question and then not even listen to the answer. Like he didn't care what the answer was… He would wake up, come in here, and he would say, "Hallo there, princess," and I would not even turn around to look at him.

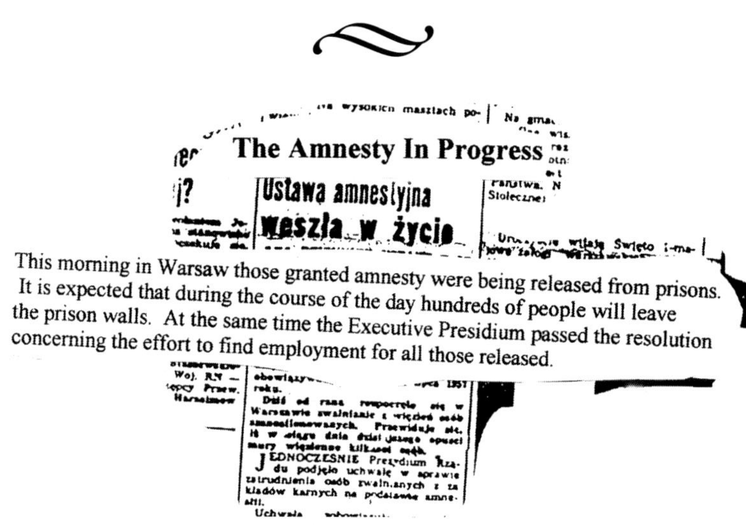

The Amnesty In Progress

This morning in Warsaw those granted amnesty were being released from prisons. It is expected that during the course of the day hundreds of people will leave the prison walls. At the same time the Executive Presidium passed the resolution concerning the effort to find employment for all those released.

I heard the door to the big room open, and I felt him looking at me. I lowered my head and pretended to be very busy coloring. For awhile he was silent, and then he said, "You remember I used to call you princess, don't you?"

"I don't think I remember, but Mama said you did," I answered, still working intently at my drawing.

"So is this the way a beautiful princess greets her father, the king?"

"I was a very young child then. Now I'm almost thirteen," I reminded him.

"I understand; you're no longer a child, and so we can't play childish games anymore. Then let's start from the beginning. Hello there, young miss!"

"Hello!" I said.

He hesitated a moment and then shuffled to the gas range in silence. I took a quick look at him and back to my notebook. He had a beard that was half black and half gray, and he was very skinny. He was wearing his old, plaid, flannel pajama pants and an undershirt, which had holes under the arms.

"And why aren't you at school this morning, young miss?" he asked.

"It's a state holiday," I explained. "Mr. Zalewski said that Proletariat is celebrating its independence, and all schools and factories and offices are celebrating too. What about prisons? Are prisons celebrating?"

"Who's Mr. Zalewski?"

"He's our principal," I said, "and you didn't answer me if the prisons are celebrating." I wanted to make him angry; I wanted him to yell at me, tell me to shut up, or slam the door, or do something to make me cry. Instead, he bent over the pot of oatmeal and banged on its sides with the wooden spoon.

"I have no way of knowing about prisons since I'm not there anymore," he finally said. "I'm here now…this is my home." He was stirring the oatmeal, and for awhile we said nothing.

"Would you like some oatmeal, young miss, or have you outgrown that as well?"

"I already had my oatmeal with Mama this morning," I said. "We eat very early, then she meets Fishel, and they take daily paper deliveries at five thirty. Only today he didn't come. Mama wouldn't let him…because of you."

He was walking like a mummy, carrying a bowl of oatmeal to the table. When I said "Fishel," he stopped and looked at me. I pretended not to know he was watching me. I was afraid to look him in the eye and find the dark, scary emptiness Sophie's father had in his eyes when he came back, one step away from something unspeakable.

"Fishel?" he repeated. "Is he still hanging around? What's he doing?"

I bit my lower lip and fiercely tried to concentrate on coloring the umbrella. The way he asked about Fishel made me think I shouldn't say any more because it would make him angry with Mama or Fishel. I wanted him to be angry, but I wanted him to be angry with *me*. I wanted him to be unhappy and feel unwelcomed. I wanted him to be sorry he came back. This was to be his punishment for lying and for leaving.

"He comes by…sometimes," I said softly. "He takes me to the movies or brings us chicken for dinner. Mama says he probably steals it somewhere, but I don't mind."

For a moment my mind wandered. I thought about the taste of Fishel's chicken when Mama made it with onions, and my mouth kept on talking, all by itself. Mama always said that when I kept on talking without even knowing what I was saying, I usually got in trouble.

"Maybe he'll bring one today…" I went on, "but no, Mama said he won't be coming around…for awhile… It's because you're here."

The steam was rising from his oatmeal, but he just stood there in silence, holding the back of the chair.

"You like chicken?" he finally said after a long pause.

"Sure do, with onions. And you?"

"I do too," he said. "I just don't know if I like it well enough when it comes from Fishel."

"You think he steals it, don't you? But Mama is just teasing him like that, and he teases Mama back, saying we will all be arrested for being acces—something or other, because we ate it."

He sat down heavily and reached for the bowl of sugar. He took a heaping spoon but instead of sprinkling it on his oatmeal, he watched the sugar crystals fall off the spoon back into the bowl. He was not listening anymore. He was thinking of something else.

"So, Mama and Fishel just go on like this, teasing each other back and forth?" he said.

"No, they don't. Sometimes they fight. And it's about you."

"About me?" he asked evidently surprised. "What do they say about me?"

"All I know is that Mama starts crying and runs out of the house, and Fishel grabs her sweater and runs after her. Sometimes I just hear Mama in the stairwell, yelling at him to stay away and leave her alone."

He leaned forward across the table and asked, "What d'you do then? You follow them on the staircase?"

"Nope. I take my notebook and draw Chinese pictures."

He fell back in his chair. "Chinese pictures?" he said. "What are Chinese pictures?"

"The pictures on the vase. See? Here."

He rose from his chair and shuffled from the other end of the table to the kitchen window. He dragged his slippers as if he didn't know how to wear them. When he leaned over me to look at the vase and my notebook, he was very close. I cringed and moved away because of his sour smell. I said:

"Mama says that before the war, the red robe and this vase belonged to Grandma Aniela."

"Grandma…yeah," he said, "she was crazy about the vase. All through the war she had it wrapped up in blankets. During every air raid she took it with her to the basement. People thought she was nuts. Everyone else took food and water and maybe a blanket, but Grandma—no—she took Chinese porcelain!"

"Did she give it to you before she died?" I asked.

"Never mind the vase," he said sharply. "What about Mama and Fishel when they're fighting on the staircase?"

I really felt uncomfortable taking about Mama and Fishel and was glad when our talk turned to Grandma Aniela and her vase.

"Why do you keep asking me questions about Mama and Fishel?" I said. "Is it because you don't like my answers?"

There was a loud knock on the door, and he jumped away from me and turned to the door. He looked pale and frightened.

"Who can it be so early in the morning?" he asked.

I didn't know why, but he was whispering, so I went along and whispered back to him.

"Oh, it's probably just Mrs. Oggler. She sometimes comes by to check if I had breakfast."

Again he leaned toward me and whispered, "Mrs. who?"

"Mrs. Marta Oggler," I said. "She lives right above us on the third floor. She has a white kitten I play with."

Whoever it was at the door was getting impatient, and the knocking got louder. Still he didn't seem to be in a hurry to open the door. He was whispering again, so I had to come up still closer to him because over the racket at the door, I could barely hear what he was saying.

"What does she want with us?" I heard him ask.

"All she wants is to see you, sort of check you out. Mama told her you are—were—in prison, and Mrs. Oggler is a person who likes to check things out. She likes to know about things. All kinds of things."

I was not even sure if it was Mrs. Oggler at the door, but whoever it was, he or she was getting very annoyed. The banging on the door went on while he stood helplessly in the middle of the kitchen. When I was home with Mama and someone was at the door, she usually told me to go and see who was it or went to open it herself. With him I didn't know what to do. I was about to go to the door when, after several extra hard blows, Mrs. Oggler's voice bellowed from the other side.

"Agnes? Do you hear me? Open up! I know you're in there, Agnes! Open up this minute!"

Still he didn't seem to realize we needed to do something. In a whisper he told me not to let Mrs. Oggler in. But I knew I had to.

"She's Mama's best friend, and she takes care of me when Mama's at the stand," I whispered back. I looked at him for some sign of what he wanted me to do, but I saw he was confused and maybe even afraid. And all the while Mrs. Oggler was whacking at the door. I was sure she wouldn't quit until I let her in.

"Coming, Mrs. Oggler!" I yelled.

On tiptoes he ran to the big room and closed the door behind him. Mrs. Oggler was mad. Her face was red all over, and her strawberry nose looked like it was about to burst. She was carrying two canvas bags full of something, and she could not fit in the door. Puffing, she turned sideways to get herself and her bags through. She was so mad she was gasping for breath.

"Whoosh! What's the big idea of keeping me out for such a time? So, where is he?" she asked.

"He's getting dressed. Let me close the front door, Mrs. Oggler, and I'll go fetch him."

I said these things loud enough so that he could hear me through the door. I was not sure he would come out on his own. I left Mrs. Oggler in the kitchen. She'd get busy checking what was in the pots and in my notebook. When I brought him out, she was doing just that. In the meantime, he managed to put on an old, stretched-out sweater, which Fishel used sometimes, but was still wearing his pajama pants. Mrs. Oggler stepped back, folded her hands on the top of her belly, and looked him over from head to toe.

"The jailbird—heh, heh!" She laughed. "The enemy of the people—look at him, holy Mother of Jesus! You did time for the black market, eh? What did you do? Drink a little vodka, play a little poker, and sell a few cartons of imperialistic cigarettes? You small time hood! You amateur! I've been in this business ever since the war ended, but I'm serious about it. And you? You had yourself a little good time, made a little money, and what? You left a fine woman and daughter alone, with no money, no help, no nothing. What's a poor woman to do? She gets this sad, skinny Jew to come around. Shame, such shame!"

While Mrs. Oggler was still talking, he made two steps backward, and then he said, "What do you want from me? I don't even know you! "

"But I know you and the likes of you!" Mrs. Oggler was yelling in a high pitched voice and moving closer. "Janie, such a fine, hard-working woman, from mornin' till night in that cold shack with these newspapers. All for this little one and to send you food packages to the slammer! For good women always bad luck with men! Men like you!"

Oh, my God, I thought. I'd never seen Mrs. Oggler worked up like that. Flailing arms, wagging fingers. And he seemed to be getting angry at her too. I wished Mama would come home. *Maybe I can run and get her. Oh, gosh…*

"You have no right to speak to me like that." Suddenly his voice sounded different, as if it came from another person. "My wife is not here, and you have no business being here. Please get out! Get out of my house! Get out now! "

Mrs Oggler spread out her arms and made her appeal to heaven: "May Saint Teresa, the patron of patience, be my witness! He's throwing me out! Me—who saved his kin from starvation while he played farting contests with them, other convicts!"

I thought Mrs. Oggler had gone mad with anger. She was crossing herself, pounding her chest, and poking him in the chest with her finger. He was retreating until his back was against the wardrobe. Suddenly he lunged at her and yelled at the top of his lungs. His voice came out all squeaky, like woman's voice. *Oh, my God! They're going to kill each other!*

"Out, out! You old, fat, screeching hag!" he yelled.

"Oh, please, please stop!" I pleaded with him. "Mrs. Oggler, you too! Please stop screaming and go now. Please, both of you just stop! Stop right now!"

I pushed myself right between them, pounding their bellies and chests with my fists. I was so afraid of dying! Of him dying, Mrs. Oggler dying, myself…

"Stoooop noooow!" I screamed at the top of my lungs.

Mrs. Oggler stepped back. There was silence. I felt so stupid and so small between the two of them. It seemed they both felt awkward too. Mrs. Oggler picked up her bags and said:.

"May I rot in hell for eternity if my foot ever touches this threshold again. And, you"—she turned to Father—"do everyone a favor. Go back where you came from!"

She maneuvered herself and her bags through the door, and he slammed the door behind her. I was all shaky, and although I wasn't crying, there were tears running down my face. I felt sorry for Mama, for Fishel, and for Mrs. Oggler, who wasn't coming back, and for myself, and even for him, who stood hunched by the door and didn't look at all like a father is supposed to look. By now my nose was stuffed because of all the tears, and I hated that.

"She called Fishel a skinny Jew, and now she won't let me play with her kitten, and we won't get any more fresh eggs or meat from her. See what you've done!" I said.

"What have I done?" he asked.

Uncle Henry was not very tall, heavy set, and wide in the shoulders. But his moves were surprisingly quick. Long ago he was a soccer player. He often said that when he was young he used to run after the ball, but now he was the coach, so he could tell others to do the running. Uncle Henry was the coach of our national team, which made him very important. Every once in awhile when he came to visit, people stopped him in our stairwell to talk to him about different players on the team or about different games. He always had tickets to the games to give away to friends. Sometimes he gave them away to total strangers. That was the way Uncle Henry was. He liked to give things away. And he wanted everyone to like him.

Once when we went to see a game, Fishel told Mama that Uncle Henry could have been a star player if he were less emotional and stayed off the booze.

"What do you mean?" Mama asked.

"Henry has a soul of a poet," Fishel explained. "When he feels good, he drinks a few to celebrate life. But vodka makes him sad, and when he's sad, he cries. When he's depressed, naturally, he drinks to elevate his spirits. But it never helps because he always has the same reaction to vodka—it makes him sad, and he cries."

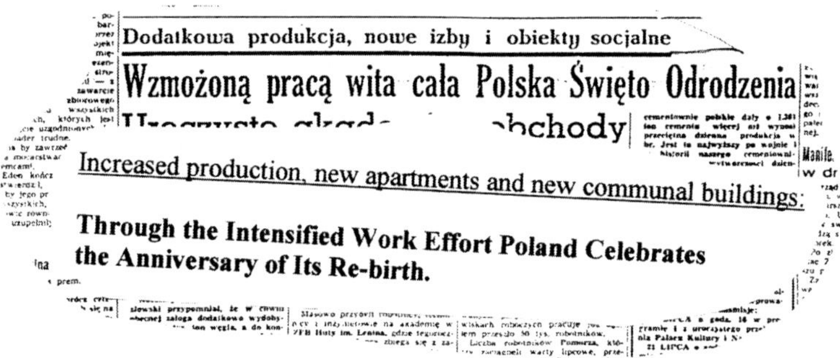

When I came home from the Independence Day parade, Uncle Henry was already in tears. He was sitting with Father at the round table in the big room, wiping his eyes with a corner of the blue, checkered tablecloth, which was permanently stained with tea and tomato soup. On the table, besides a half empty bottle of vodka, there were four glasses, a plate of herring in sour cream, some bread, and my Chinese vase and notebook.

I guessed that Mama, needing more room in the kitchen, moved the vase and the notebook out of the way. Then, because of the vodka and the herring, they were moved again, all the way to the side of the round table.

Uncle Henry had put his arm around Father's shoulders and was tearfully trying to reassure him, "It's good to have you back, Theo! We're so happy… Rita!" He called out to Aunt Rita who was helping Mama in the kitchen. "Aren't we happy he's back home? Tell him, tell him, Rita…"

"Oh, knock it off, Henry," she yelled. "You've already had way too much of your juice. Stay off the vodka for a while until we get some food ready. You can't hold booze on the empty stomach."

Ignoring Aunt Rita's angry voice, Uncle Henry proposed a toast. "To your health, Theo…" And after a moment of hesitation he added, "…and to the health of comrade Stalin."

"But Uncle Henry," I said, "Comrade Stalin is dead."

"So he is…so he is…and in this case, he needs it even more so."

"Henry Korsak," Aunt Rita said, coming in with a plate of steaming sausage. "Mind your tongue and your drink! Oh my! Aggie! Aren't you soaked! What happened?"

"We got caught in the rain, waiting for a bus," I explained.

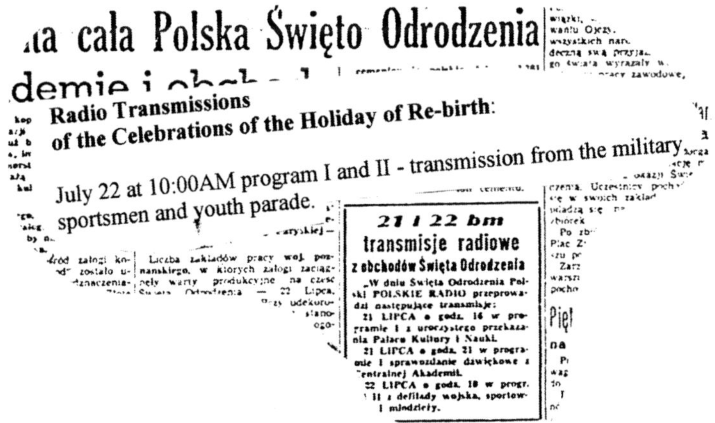

Aunt Rita placed the plate of sausage in front of Father and Uncle Henry. "Let me have that jacket. I'll hang it the kitchen. It'll dry faster. You go on and change." She pushed me in the direction of the bathroom.

In a dry, long-sleeved top, I still felt cold. The kitchen was a nice, warm, and steamy, food-smelling place. Mama was cutting pickles.

"Can I have one?"

"Come to the table. We all have dinner together," she said.

"I'll be bored, and the smell of vodka will make me sick."

"Let her eat here, Janie," Aunt Rita intervened. She was always on my side. Among the grownups, she was my best buddy, my favorite. I got a piece of sausage, a pickle, and a slice of bread with margarine. I ate the pickle first, watching through the window the rings drops of rain made on the surface of puddles. I wondered why people drank vodka. It made them silly, and the smell was sickening. Aunt Rita always laughed too loud, Uncle Henry cried for no reason, and Mama tried to make sure she pronounced every word correctly and spoke so slowly it drove me bonkers. I couldn't remember what Father usually did when he drank too much vodka, but I was sure I'd know before this dinner was over.

"What happened to the place on Sienna Street?" I heard him ask.

"First they searched it and turned everything upside down. Then they locked it. Put a big padlock on the gate and a notice that it's off limits because it's a part of the 'government case against the antisocial elements," said Aunt Rita.

"That's us," Father said, "…and Przemek, and Fishel, and the rest…all elements."

"Let's drink to that," said Uncle Henry.

I wanted another pickle. I was standing in the door of the big room, trying to get Mama's attention. Uncle Henry was rocking back and forth in his chair. The whole room was already filled with the sour, suffocating smell of vodka. I didn't want to go in any farther, but Mama was not looking my way.

"Fishel…" Father said, and his voice trailed off. Then he added, "I could wring his neck."

"You wouldn't have said that if you knew how much he had helped your wife," said Aunt Rita.

"You mean how he had helped himself to my wife."

"I can see Henry's been busy putting some twisted ideas in your head," said Mama.

Father looked intently at his glass filled with vodka. There must have been something either on the bottom of the glass or maybe floating in it.

"Not only Henry. It's Mrs. Oggler and even Agnes. Fishel's name just keeps popping up in all sorts of conversations. For all I know, I'm probably sitting in his chair and wearing his sweater." He emptied his glass and poured himself another one.

Mama watched him and then she said, "Henry is sitting in his chair. But you're right about the sweater." She got up from the table so abruptly her chair tipped over and fell to the floor.

This was not a good time to ask her for a pickle. No one even knew I was in the doorway. They were always trying to be different when they knew I was around, as if they wanted to hide things from me. So I stayed quiet.

Mama leaned across the table. "Go ahead, Theo," she said, "Go ahead, get drunk! Feel sorry for yourself! God, what a cheap melodrama!" She was angry, and her voice was getting louder.

"He comes home from prison a broken man," she said, "and his wife, instead of waiting for him, had taken a younger lover, and they are both corrupting his only child. Here's your story, Theo. Now you have an excuse. You can tell it to every drunk in every bar. You've always needed an excuse to do what you want. Isn't that the truth, Theo? Isn't that the truth?" Aunt Rita picked up her chair, and she sat down heavily, all out of breath.

I knew I was the child, and the lover was Fishel. It was like a play about Uncle Vania our class went to see last year. Only it wasn't about rich landowners and poor peasants Mrs. Pawlak told us about. It was about a man in love with somebody else's wife. All the people in the play were real, and I kept dreaming about them for weeks. My dreams were very beautiful, and although no one died, somehow, they were also very sad.

I decided I wanted to see the rest of this play, the one taking place in our big room, at the table. I slipped behind the door from where I could see all the actors, except Aunt Rita, through the crack between the hinges. Mama was all out of breath after yelling about the truth. Now it was Father's turn. He leaned back in his chair and said, "It's you who's looking for an excuse, blaming me for getting caught. Do you want to kick me out, or would you rather have both of us in your bed?"

Mama dropped her fork onto the plate. She was about to say something to Father when Uncle Henry intervened:

"Leave him be, Janie. The man just got out of the slammer, wanted to celebrate a bit with his brother, his best buddy! All he needs now is a loving woman to make him some coffee and put him to bed." Aunt Rita got up. She was looking around for her purse. She was ready to leave.

"Henry, you stay out of it!" she said. "Get your jacket, and let's go home." But Uncle Henry was not about to leave while the bottle of vodka was still half full.

"I'm not going anywhere," he said. "I'm not leaving my brother with a man-eating barracuda." Mama was the 'man-eating barracuda' and Uncle Henry was in trouble. She looked at him with disgust and said:

"You're drunk, Henry. If it weren't for your wife, I'd have you out the door in no time."

Uncle Henry was digging himself into a still deeper hole: "I can't let you abuse my best buddy"—he was patting Father's back—"telling him he's unfit to be a father...or a husband!"

Mama rose, pushed her chair away and yelled at Uncle Henry, Father, and all the other men in the world: "Oh…you! You're all unfit! You, Fishel, Theo, and the rest! For all of you everything begins and ends in bed. You can't see beyond the end of your… nose! I'm not blaming Theo just for getting caught. It was inevitable. I knew it was coming. From the beginning I did not like this entire business. The business and everything that came with it: the men, the hours, the drinking, the card games, the secrecy, and the fear that someone will see or hear. You, Theo, looking for steady work, working regular hours? Who were you kidding?" Now Mama paced up and down the room as if she were going over her next lines in her head.

"What do you know about looking for work?" asked Father looking at the wall across from him as if he didn't care who he was talking to, "about the responsibility for others hanging over your head, about not being of use…to anyone? What did it matter to you how I got the money, as long as there was enough to buy food, pay rent, and get new shoes for Agnes?"

Mama stopped pacing. She looked straight at him and said, "You're not listening to me, Theo, or you choose not to understand. What I'm trying to say is that now is the time to clean up our lives. You'll have to decide whether or not you'll stop drinking and how you're going to make your living from now on. How you make money has an influence on how we live, and I want to have something to say about it. This may be the only chance I will ever have to consider whether or not I want you back in our lives."

Father tried to get up. He had to hold onto the table for balance. His face turned red. He was very angry. "Sit down, Janie! Sit down and tell me how you want to clean up your life. Who and what you want to keep and whom you want to discard. You want me to stop drinking and clean up my life too, don't you? All right! We may as well start here!"

He swept everything off the table. Food flew in the air, bottles, glasses, dishes, the Chinese vase, and my notebook all landed in a heap on the floor. Everything was broken. Uncle Henry jumped away from the table. His chair fell back on the floor. Even though Uncle Henry was very fast, some herring and sour cream ended up on his pants.

"Jesus Christ, Theo!" cried Uncle Henry. "What on earth did you do that for? Look at this mess! Look what you've done to my good pants! Rita, get some boiling water! Does sour cream come off with boiling water?"

Uncle Henry stretched his pants to the sides, trying to prevent further spreading of the globs of sour cream, which were stuck around his fly. Slowly, on stiff legs, wobbling from side to side, he moved like a penguin toward the kitchen. Mama pushed Father away from the table. "Cut it out, Theo! Enough!" she said loudly. "Good Lord, your mother's vase and all these dishes. How are we going to replace these?"

This was the end of the play because now I was crying. Mama was crying too. She knelt down to examine the pieces. I wanted to help her pick them up. I wanted her to hold me. On the way to the other side of the table, I passed by Father, who was saying, "Oh, God, the vase! I broke the vase!"

Aunt Rita, who seemed to be the only sane person in this room, looked at the ceiling and said, "Thou shalt not take the name of the Lord thy God in vain!"

The Crocodile and the Swamp Master

"It's so unfair to be sick during school vacation, isn't it?" said Aunt Rita. I must have gotten this cold when we were caught in a storm on the twenty-second of July, which was the Independence Day. Aunt Rita kicked off her sandals and made herself comfortable at the other end of my bed. I didn't mind being sick when she was the one who watched over me. Besides Mama, Aunt Rita and Fishel were my favorite people.

Aunt Rita was very pretty. Mama said that she had dark complexion, which looked like she always had a suntan, even in the middle of winter. She also had dark, curly hair. I wished I had hair like Aunt Rita, falling around my face in soft little ringlets. She had married Uncle Henry not too long ago because even I could remember their wedding. She looked like a picture from the fashion magazine in a cream-colored suit and a small hat the size of a candy box, which covered only one of her ears. At the wedding, Grandma T. said Aunt Rita married Uncle Henry so that she could buy more clothes. Mama told Grandma T. not to be jealous of Aunt Rita because Uncle Henry was not her son. I think Grandma T. was just doing what she did best, which was being a sourpuss.

Aunt Rita had always been very nice to Mama, but Mama liked Mrs. Oggler better. After father came home and broke almost all of our dishes, Aunt Rita had given us some of her cups, saucers, and plates. It was her dishes we used every day from then on because Mama didn't have the money to buy us the new ones.

We were going to play cards, and Aunt Rita doled them out on to the blanket I was under, but instead of picking up our hands, we talked about the women at her work. I knew all about them because she always told me stories about their boyfriends, husbands, and children. I knew who was in love with whom, and who was going to have a baby. There was even one woman in her office whose daughter had eloped with a Russian officer because her folks wouldn't let her marry him. The daughter now lived somewhere called Odessa, where it was very warm all the time, and palm trees grew in the streets.

Aunt Rita worked for the National Sports Agency and, I guess, because Uncle Henry coached the national soccer team, this was how they met. I asked Aunt Rita to tell me again how Uncle Henry kept sneaking chocolates into her desk at the office when she wasn't looking, how he had his friends call her away from her desk so that he could do it, and how she wondered for weeks who her secret admirer was. She was just getting to the good part, how she caught him, when we heard someone knocking on the front door. Aunt Rita went to see who it was, and from my bed I heard her talking to a man, but I didn't recognize his voice. She came back, holding a large, white envelope.

"Who was it?" I asked.

"Remember Pan Wladek, the militiaman who used to play poker with your father?" In my mind I immediately saw Pan Wladek, but not playing poker. I saw him the night Father was arrested; he was sitting at Father's desk and going through the papers that were in the drawer. I said nothing about it to Aunt Rita. She wasn't here when it happened, so she didn't know.

"He brought this envelope," she continued. "It's addressed to your father. I thought better not to tell Pan Wladek that he had moved out. I just said he was out of town."

Because of the fever, I must have fallen asleep in the middle of our card came. When I woke up, it was already afternoon and Aunt Rita was gone. My nose was still stuffed, but I felt better. Early afternoons were usually pretty slow at the stand, so Mama often closed up for an hour or two to do shopping or to come home and quickly cook something for the evening meal. I heard the water running in the kitchen sink, which meant that she must have come in while I was asleep. I wrapped a blanket around my shoulders and went in to the kitchen to tell her about the letter.

"How do you feel, my mouse?" she asked, touching my forehead. "Your fever is down. Did Rita give you some aspirin?"

"Pan Wladek, the militiaman, was here," I said. "He brought a letter for Father. Aunt Rita put it on the table in the big room." Mama dried her hands. She examined the front and back of the envelope without opening it. She put the letter back on the table, sat down, and looked at it for a while.

Suddenly remembering about me, she said, "I need to think what to do next… In the meantime, we can eat the potato pancakes I have made. Come, you can have yours with sugar."

While we ate, she was very quiet. I supposed she was thinking about the letter and about Father. All we knew about him was that he had gone to live with Pan Przemek, one of his friends from before. Uncle Henry told us that. Father moved out the very next morning after he had broken the vase and all the dishes. I remembered that morning I had felt very sorry for him. He had slept the night with all his clothes on and looked really wretched. His hair was all messed up, standing straight on the top and stuck to his skull on the sides. He came out of the room, holding his head as if it was about to explode into tiny fragments.

"Where does your mama keep aspirin and coffee?" he asked. I was at the table, trying to put together the pieces of the Chinese vase he had broken the night before. Mama and I had picked up all the pieces and put them in the empty shoebox.

"Coffee's in a tin can on the top shelf," I said, "and aspirin you can't have. It's for sick people." I heard him rummaging through the shelves in the kitchen.

"Are you still drunk?" I asked when he came in to the room. "I don't want you to come here and knock the table and wreck all these pieces again."

"No, I'm not drunk," he said, irritated. "Now I'm sick. So where's that aspirin?"

"In a large medicine jar next to the coffee," I said and then added, "I've never seen a grown man break dishes before."

He looked at me and said very quietly, "It happens when a man is scared and doesn't know what to do next. He tries to cover up the fear, and then he does silly things like getting drunk and breaking dishes."

He said all this not to me but to a coffeepot he was holding in his hand. Still, it almost made me cry. Grownups never admitted they were afraid, as if it were a childish thing to do.

"Were you scared last night?" I asked him just to make sure that was what he had said.

"I guess so," he answered, still not looking at me. "You know, you'll need special glue to hold these pieces together." He pointed to the shoebox. "When I have the money, I'll get you the glue."

"What were you scared of?" I asked.

He took a sip of the coffee and said very softly, "That your mama will leave me."

Again I was getting all choked up, so I pretended to rummage in the box for a new piece. "She can't go anywhere," I said. "She would have to take me with her, and I have to go to confession tomorrow. Besides, we don't even own a suitcase that is big enough."

He finally looked at me and smiled. "This is a very strange situation," he said, "but in order for your mama to leave me, it is I who has to pack up and go." I heard him swallow the coffee.

"Are you going too?" I asked.

He didn't answer but brought out his black bag and started throwing in his stuff.

"I'm borrowing Fishel's sweater. Mine has holes on the elbows," he said.

Mama opened the letter that evening after dinner. She said she needed to see if there were any deadlines in it and how much time she had to get a hold of Father. It turned out that inside it was addressed to both Mama and Father.

"May I look at it?" I asked. The piece of paper she handed me looked very official. It had a round, red stamp under the signature.

> Citizens Theodore Korsak and Janina Korsak:
>
> The Central Bureau of State Security needs your immediate assistance in a matter of great urgency. Your civic duty requires that you appear on July 27th, 1953, 9:00 a.m. (Room 022) at 56 Krucza Street. Please bring this letter with you.
>
> Lieutenant Ignacy Kuc
> Senior Investigator

I wondered why there was so much talk and apprehension about a message so simple and straightforward. Uncle Henry and Aunt Rita came by later that night. They also wanted to know what was in the letter. They were all very worried that it had been hand delivered by Pan Wladek and not mailed. Uncle Henry said we had to be careful because this might be a *provocation* (later I looked it up in a dictionary but couldn't figure out how it fit in with the letter).

Mama repeatedly questioned Aunt Rita what Pan Wladek said when he gave it to her, but it didn't really mean anything. Finally they decided that Uncle Henry would try to get a hold of Father and tell him what was going on, and in the meantime, Mama would go to the security bureau by herself on the appointed day to see if she could find out what they wanted from us. She was going to tell them that Father needed a rest and was visiting his other brother, Uncle Bert, who lived on the outskirts of the city.

Although everyone seemed to be very nervous about this letter, especially Mama, to me it seemed like an exciting mystery. Since Father moved out, Fishel stopped coming, I'd gotten sick, and my life had become terribly boring. All I could do was read, color, or try to put the Chinese vase back together. Putting the vase together was in some ways like a puzzle but not as good because without the glue it couldn't be finished.

It was the third day of my cold. I finally had no fever, and I was feeling much better. I was really anxious to get out of the house and play outside.

"How would you like to keep me company tomorrow when I go to the State Security Bureau?" Mama asked me at dinner. At first I was sort of disappointed because I want to play in the courtyard with the other kids while she was gone, but on second thought, not too many kids I knew could boast of having been to the State Security Bureau. I could even say I had been summoned together with my mama and make it sound more important.

There was no official government insignia on the building on Krucza Street. It was just a plain office building, like so many others lining the streets of the city. The downstairs waiting room was filled with people, and the cigarette smoke was so thick I started coughing and couldn't stop, although everyone, even the woman in the window wearing a uniform, was sternly looking at me. When it was our turn, Mama gave the woman in the window the letter, and she led us down two flights of stairs into the bowels of the building.

Mama and I, we always went through the same routine whenever she took me along somewhere. I kept looking around, dragging my feet, and tripping over everything imaginable, and she was impatient, tugging at my hand, and cursing herself for taking me with her in the first place. This time we were faithfully following our routine step by step when we arrived in front of the room number twenty-two. The door to the room was padded and covered with thick brown leather. The woman leading us through the basement maze opened it without knocking, showed us in, and closed it behind us. A tall, skinny, bold man was standing by the window with his back turned to us. He was talking on the telephone. Actually, what I saw was only a receiver at his ear because the rest of the telephone was hidden in the drawer of his desk. The long cord coming out of the drawer was connecting this man's ear to his desk. I thought it was sort of funny. I also wondered why a person would want to hide a telephone inside a desk. I was about to ask Mama what she thought might be the reason when the man turned, motioned us to sit down, and then continued with his conversation. There were two chairs side by side, one for Mama and one for me. On the other side of a large empty desk there was a bigger, black chair for the man. While he was still talking on the telephone, I asked Mama where all the important papers and documents were, which people who work in offices usually read and write. Aunt Rita said that's what they did in her office. And, of course, in her office they stamped the most important documents with red ink. Once Aunt Rita brought this important stamp for me to play with, just for one evening. The stamp said, "*CONFIDENTIAL*," which really meant, "*It's a secret.*" But Mama was in no mood for talking. She just wanted to sit and wait.

When the man was finally finished, he put the receiver and the cord back into the drawer and then introduced himself.

"I'm Lieutenant Kuc, and I know who you are. I'm surprised to see Miss…Agnes…yes, Miss Agnes here, instead of her father," he said, sitting down in his big chair. The chair squeaked loudly and the sound surprised Lieutenant Kuc. He looked down at it as if checking if it was going to hold up. He tried to pull it up closer to the desk, but it squeaked again. Now Lieutenant Kuc looked annoyed.

"This matter is confidential; that's why I'm surprised to see Miss Agnes here instead of your husband," he said to Mama.

"Agnes is a serious girl, quite grown up for her age. She understands what should and should not be discussed in public," said Mama to my great amazement.

I was really astonished that Mama thought I was *quite grown up for my age.* Especially since she so often told me that I would understand some things when I grow up. Since the last time we talked about it, I did not seem to understand any more things than I did before.

"Very well," said Lieutenant Kuc. "Still, it's very unfortunate Citizen Korsak isn't here." The chair squeaked in agreement. Lieutenant Kuc cleared his throat. "It came to our attention that one of the rooms in your apartment faces the courtyard and is directly opposite premises occupied by the suspect, counterrevolutionary elements. We believe these individuals to be engaged in the anti-state activities, which need to be monitored and, at the proper moment, prevented. Your family—Citizen Korsak in particular—should be grateful to this government for its leniency and should be anxious to assist us in any way you can. To assure your security and security of other citizens from foreign meddling and intervention, this government needs your assistance now." Lieutenant Kuc leaned back in his chair, and it promptly squeaked signaling the end of his speech.

This entire time Mama was sitting straight up, at the edge of her seat. She was very tense. "What exactly do you want us to do?" she asked.

"We do not force our citizens and comrades to do anything. We expect them to assist us because they feel it's their civic duty." Lieutenant Kuc spoke very evenly, without stressing certain words more than others, as if he didn't care what he was saying.

"And how can we assist our government?" Mama asked.

"Well, that's better," said Lieutenant Kuc. "We will help you fulfill your civic duty. One of our officers with a transmitter will be placed in that room of yours. He or she will observe the suspect individuals and report their activities. I'll personally make sure we'll assign women officers for the evening and night shifts. Citizen Korsak, I salute your family's sacrifice of your privacy for the cause of state security!"

"How long will this go on?" asked Mama, looking at the tips of her shoes.

"At the present stage in our investigation, it's hard to tell, but I'd say a month or so." Lieutenant Kuc shifted his weight, and the chair squeaked again. Mama rose from her seat and was standing in front of his desk, tightly squeezing her purse. Her knuckles were shining white against the brown leather.

"I'll think about it and let you know. We need to have some time. I have to talk to Theo…my husband." Mama put her hand on my shoulder and lightly urged me to turn around.

We were almost at the door when Lieutenant Kuc said, "I'm saying this not as an officer of the bureau but as a private citizen. My advice is to do the state a favor. It's good to have at least one thing in your plus column in case you someday trip and fall."

I didn't understand the last part about tripping and falling. It must be one of these messages meant to be "*CONFIDENTIAL.*" I was going to ask Mama about it later.

From the bureau, we went directly to Mama's stand. Fishel was there filling in for her. I was excited at the prospect of seeing him again. It's been more than a week since I last talked to him. During the ride on the bus, I was very quiet and on my best behavior; I knew that although Mama looked calm to other people, inside she was really furious. There was his deep furrow between her eyebrows, and her lips were so tight they looked just like a thin, sharp cut across her face. When we got off the bus and I saw Fishel at the stand, I couldn't stop myself from running to hug him. He lifted me up and together we spun with me flying in the air. I told him to put me down because after what Mama had said to Lieutenant Kuc about me, I felt I was too grown up to do this kind of stuff.

"What's up, your highness?" he asked me, but Mama caught up with us, and I had no chance to tell him about the vase, or that Father had moved out and he could come to visit. Mama went directly inside the stand and threw her purse into the corner with such force that it broke open and everything spilled out. A small round mirror she sometimes used to fix her hair cracked into three pieces. Mrs. Wyglondalo once told me that broken mirror meant bad luck, and the number of pieces into which it was broken meant how many years the bad luck was going to last. But Mama was not paying attention to the mirror.

"Now, after Theo's foul up, they think they own us. Or maybe they thought that all along but were not as blunt about it as they are now," she said.

"What did they want?" asked Fishel.

"After what happened to Theo, it doesn't seem like much. They just want to use one of our rooms to spy on some people across the courtyard. That's all." She opened and shut the drawer under the counter for no reason.

"Can't you just say no?" asked Fishel.

"How can we refuse to do our 'civic duty' to redeem ourselves in the eyes of the state? Oh, God, I've had enough of this you call 'precious gift of life!'" She covered her face, and her shoulders quivered. I put my arms around her hips and held her very tightly. She was crying, and her voice came muffled through her hands.

"I will let them in, and they'll spy on the other people through our window, and they'll spy on us from the inside of our own home. We won't be able to talk or to listen to the London broadcast or to have friends come and tell us anti-government jokes. I'll have to teach Agnes how to talk without saying anything, and we'll have no refuge from their eyes and their ears. How can we live like that?"

After what Mama had said to Fishel, I realized that the officers of the bureau who were to sit day and night in out apartment were really spies watching someone else in our building. The chills went down my spine. It was both scary and thrilling. At night, in the dark, I speculated as to who were the people across the courtyard the bureau spies would be watching, and how "counterrevolution-ary elements" really looked. I was also kind of sorry I would not be able to tell any of my friends we had real spies sitting in our small room. This was "CONFIDENTIAL." What also surprised me was how much listening occasionally to the London Broadcast and exchanging anti-government jokes meant to Mama, Father, and all the others who came to visit us. As far as I was concerned, the only fun thing about the broadcast was the signal, the deep, resonant sound of bum, bum, bum, bum that came over the radio waves. The rest was really boring. There was a lot of crackling and static, the voices seemed to drift away into space, then comeback for a few seconds and drift away again. Everyone crowded around the radio to hear better, but there was no use. They were never sure what they actually heard, so after it ended they mostly compared what each one got out of it. "The bottom line is," Father said, "that the communists are getting better and better interfering with the incoming radio waves and pretty soon they'll cut us off altogether."

The following Monday when I came back from the religion class, Fishel was again at the stand, and Mama was home waiting for me. The door to the small room was shut. All my books and games and toys had been moved to the big room. They were on the floor in a big heap. Mama put her finger across her lips and in silence motioned me to the kitchen.

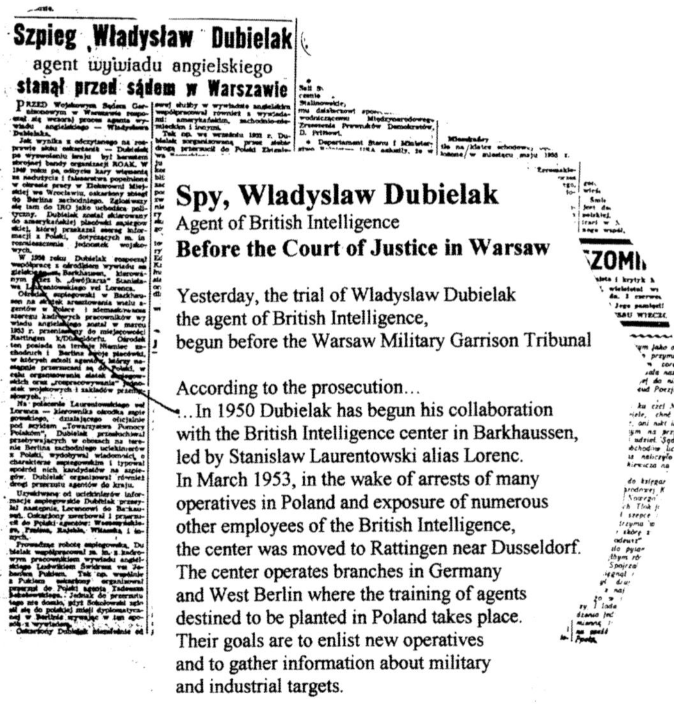

Szpieg ,Władysław Dubielak
agent wywiadu angielskiego
stanął przed sądem w Warszawie

Spy, Wladyslaw Dubielak
Agent of British Intelligence
Before the Court of Justice in Warsaw

Yesterday, the trial of Wladyslaw Dubielak
the agent of British Intelligence,
begun before the Warsaw Military Garrison Tribunal

According to the prosecution...
...In 1950 Dubielak has begun his collaboration
with the British Intelligence center in Barkhaussen,
led by Stanislaw Laurentowski alias Lorenc.
In March 1953, in the wake of arrests of many
operatives in Poland and exposure of numerous
other employees of the British Intelligence,
the center was moved to Rattingen near Dusseldorf.
The center operates branches in Germany
and West Berlin where the training of agents
destined to be planted in Poland takes place.
Their goals are to enlist new operatives
and to gather information about military
and industrial targets.

Our kitchen was very small. Trying to get through to the other end of the table with my backpack still on, I knocked the teakettle off the stove. There wasn't much water in it, but still, we both had to get down on all fours to clean it up. While we were squeezing our rags over the sink, Mama said in a very low voice, "They're in there. From now on when you come home, just get what you need for reading or play and go to Mrs. Oggler's. She'll be waiting for you. She'll also give you lunch."

I don't know what Mama said to Mrs. Oggler, but she sure was diligent and looked out for me coming from the church. She must have been watching the street through her window, which was directly above our big room, because she met me on the landing and waited while I opened the door to our apartment and got the stuff I wanted to play with. We went on like this every day until Friday, when our catechism lesson with Father Anthony was suddenly cancelled because he had tripped and fallen down the stairs. On my way home, I kept hoping Mrs. Oggler wouldn't be at her window. I knew that all along, due to Mama's pleas, Mrs. Oggler was trying to prevent me from talking to the people from the State Security Bureau. In spite of what Mama had said to Lieutenant Kuc about me, she was afraid I would accidentally say something I shouldn't. And she was probably right. Yet I wanted so badly to see, or at least hear, a real spy at work. I decided that if Mrs. Oggler were not there to stop me, I would try to take a peek.

Quietly I slipped into the hallway of our apartment, leaving the door ajar in case I had to leave in a hurry. For a while I stood in the semidarkness until my eyes adjust to the dim light and I could distinguish various objects in my path. Carefully I made my way to the door of the small room. It was closed, and the key was in the keyhole preventing me from getting a glimpse of a real spy. A few minutes passed in total silence while I was deciding what to do next. I considered giving it up for now, getting some books and going to Mrs. Oggler's when I heard a woman's voice coming through the door. What the woman said did not make any sense, so, suspecting I had missed some part of the conversation, I put my ear directly against the crack between the door and its frame.

"Crocodile Two to Swamp Master. Crocodile Two to Swamp Master. Do you hear me? Over," the spy woman said.

Then I heard a man's voice, but it sounded as if it was coming from the radio amidst the crackling and static. I guessed that must have been the 'transmitter' Lieutenant Kuc was talking about.

"This is the Swamp Master. Repeat: this is the Swamp Master. We hear you, Croc Two. What's up with the old geezer? Over." "Old geezer" must have been the man in the apartment across the courtyard.

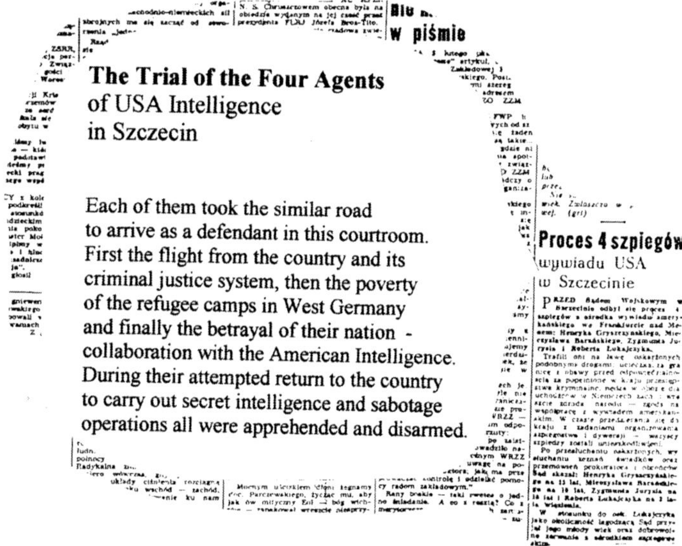

"I think he's going out. Yeah…he's buttoning up his raincoat. He's leaving… No, no, he's coming back. Wait, now he's looking for something. Behind the door…in the wardrobe…behind the wardrobe… Now he's unbuttoning his coat. He's getting the phone! He's calling someone! Do you hear me? Over," said the woman in our room.

"We hear you, Croc Two. We know he's making a phone call. We're on his line. Over." This again was the man in the "transmitter."

"Who's he calling? Over," asked the spy woman.

"American Embassy…his wife… He can't find the umbrella…" There was a long silence, and I did not hear anything.

"Are you still there, Swamp Master? Over," said the woman

"Yeah, we're still here, Crocodile Two. So what's he up to now? Over," the transmitter said.

"He's got his umbrella and his hat. Buttoning up his raincoat again. Now he's leaving. Over," reported the woman.

"Take a break, Croc Two. Crocodile One will take it from there. Over."

The Enemy

June and December were always my favorite months. December because of the Christmas tree, and June because that's when the school was finally over. August I had never liked much. I guess the return of school was already looming too close ahead. That year June, July, and also the good part of August turned out to be pretty lousy. First the news about the amnesty and Father coming home, then the breaking of the vase and Father moving out. And, to top it all off, the Crocodile sitting in my room for almost three weeks looking across the courtyard at the window of Mr. Lerkow, who was "something or other witness" and whose wife worked at the American Embassy. I was really glad when on August twenty-first the Crocodile took her suitcase "transmitter" and also moved out.

Abusing Religious Freedom
the Leaders of the Sect
"Jehovah's Witnesses"
Engaged in Anti-Polish Activities.

Recently the trail of Jan Lerkow, Wladyslaw Szklarszewicz, Tadeusz Chodara, Mieczyslaw Cyranski and Stanislaw Nabialczyk the leaders of the illegal Society of Jehovah's Witnesses was held before the Regional Court of Justice in Lodz. The defendants had close connections with foreign centers of the sect – located mainly in USA – and preyed upon religious feelings of many backward and misinformed citizens. They abused the freedom of religion to sow diversion and slander the Socialist Poland, promote the idea of the third World War and encourage evading civic responsibilities i.e. military service.

Suddenly, at the very end of the month, everything went back to how it used to be, and I liked it. Mama sold her papers every day like she used to, and I helped her sometimes in the morning. I always tried to look over the headlines to see if there was any mention of Mr. Lerkow and his wife, but I never found a thing, or maybe I missed it, because it was in a small print and hidden deeper in a paper. Until one morning when I started on an article about a religious sect. Mama said that a sect was a small group of people who practice together religion that is not very widely popular. This sect was called *Jehova's Witnesses*, and a few lines down from the beginning, Mr. Lerkow's name was at the very top of the list of people who were being tried for crimes against the State. When I pointed his name to Mama, she took the paper from my hands, sat down on the stack of papers, and read the article from top to bottom. Then she said that Mr. Lerkow in the paper wasn't our Mr. Lerkow, because our Mr. Lerkow was Leon, and the one in a paper was Jan. But I remained suspicious because before she had never even let on she knew whom the Bureau spies were watching and that she knew Mr. Lerkow's first name. I made a promise to myself to watch Mr. Lerkow's window and see if he was still there, but I got preoccupied with what was happening to Fishel and forgot all about it. Around that time Fishel started coming to visit almost every day. We even went to see a movie once, but it wasn't very good. It was a story of a partisan unit in the forest of eastern Czechoslovakia. I think they were all lost and had very little food to eat. There were many pictures of the tops of the trees and the sky beyond, and a lot of talk about the "cause." When we came out of the movie theater Fishel said, "When you can't figure out what happened in the movie, you can bet it's 'czeski film.'"

On Thursday he was helping Mama close up the stand when Mama's key got stuck in the padlock, and it wouldn't either turn or come out.

"It's time both locks should be oiled," said Fishel. The door on the side of the stand has a padlock, and the front hutch has another. He sent me home to bring some cooking oil because we didn't have any of the special kind used for machinery. Fishel always collects and keeps in his knapsack all sorts of odd things. This time he pulled out what looked like a spoke from a bicycle wheel. He stuck one end of it into the padlock and let the golden drops of oil run down along the spoke and into the keyhole. He shook the padlock and then turned the key without any effort. I was impressed.

"This should hold us over till tomorrow," he said. "Tomorrow I'll bring the can of machine oil I have at home."

But he didn't show up the next day. Mama thought nothing of it because the locks worked fine, and there were sometimes days when Fishel had other things to do, which were none of our business.

Sunday evening Mama finally said, "I've been thinking about Fishel, and I realized that we don't know where he lives. If something had happened, we wouldn't even know where to start looking for him."

The same was true about Father. Uncle Henry was the only one who knew who exactly Pan Przemek was and what was his address. Mama never asked Uncle Henry about Father, or at least not when I was around. Now and then I thought about him. It was usually when I moved the shoebox with all the pieces of the vase still in it. Now his absence was different from when he was in prison. Now he was out there, somewhere, free in the world. He could be doing many things, I thought. He could be drinking himself sick, getting arrested, or working and saving money to buy the glue that holds porcelain together. Maybe he needed someone to mend the holes on his elbows or someone to talk to when he was afraid. There were times I had wanted to ask Uncle Henry about him, but I was afraid it might upset Mama, so I didn't.

"Maybe Uncle Henry knows where Fishel is," I said.

"Well, if by tomorrow we won't hear from him, I'll ask Henry or Rita," said Mama.

She didn't get a chance to do it because the next day Fishel showed up. I was helping her to arrange the newly delivered papers. It was early in the morning and still sort of nippy. Mama said she could smell autumn in the air. I could smell school beginning on Friday. We were busy talking about the length of the pleated skirt that was a part of my uniform. I grew again this summer, and Mama had to let the hem out before Friday. Fishel quietly sneaked up behind us, and when I turned I found him just standing there, smiling, looking very pleased with himself.

"Well, look who's here!" said Mama. "We thought you went for a trip around the world and forgot to let us know."

"I went for a trip, but it wasn't that far," said Fishel. The majority of the people I knew never went on trips. Sometimes they just went to visit their relatives in another town, but that was about it.

"Where did you go?" Mama asked. But I was more interested how he got there. So far I had been on the train only once and always remembered it as an exciting event. I thought traveling by train was a very grownup and sophisticated thing to do.

"Did you go by train?" I asked him without waiting for his reply about the destination of his trip.

"To answer her highness first," he said, making a slight bow with his head in my direction, "yes, I went there by train, and it was a magical journey—full of wonder and hope. My destination was Lublin."

"Lublin? What sort of magical things can happen on the way to Lublin?" asked Mama. Her serious tone brought an end to Fishel's playfulness.

"I'm sorry," he said, "but there was no time to let you know beforehand. I had to leave immediately. Here…" Fishel reached for his backpack and from the side pocket pulled out a folded piece of paper that looked like a letter.

"Citizen Feliks Mayer, Anin forty-three…" he started reading.

"Feliks? Is that you?" Mama asked.

"All my official papers say 'Feliks,'" said Fishel. "When after the war the new government was issuing papers to the surviving Jews in Lublin, they were not in the mood to fool around with Jewish names. So I was christened on the spot. Citizen Mayer…" he started again.

"Who is it from?" I asked.

"Red Cross…"

"Red Cross!" Mama cried. "They found your baby niece! Why on earth didn't you say something from the start? Where is she?" Mama was jumping up all over Fishel, trying to get a hold of the letter while he raised it way up high, laughing and keeping it out of her reach.

"All they said was that with whatever information I gave them about the transports of Jews from Lublin to Auschwitz in 1942, and with what facts they were able to dig up on their own, all this led them to a family in Israel. The young wife is approximately our Mirah's age. My baby niece would now be twenty-one. She was born in Lublin, her name is Mirah Levy, and she has twin girls. The next step, the Red Cross people say, is up to me."

I had this sinking feeling in my stomach, which usually happened when something was about to change in a very profound way.

"What are you going to do?" I asked him so quietly that Mama turned around to look at me.

"First of all, don't get all bent out of shape, princess. Nothing's happening yet. I just had them move all the paper work from the Red Cross field office in Lublin to their local office right here. Second, when the papers arrive, they will forward, through their representative, a letter from me to Mirah Levy, verifying some details from the past, making sure she's the one. Then we will see what's next."

"I can imagine how you feel!" said Mama taking his hand.

"No, you can't know how it feels to be really alone, be cared for by no one, belong to no one, have no connection to other human beings," he said.

"Where exactly is this Israel? We better find out how to get there if you're going to live with your baby cousin, who is not a baby anymore," I said, shoving a package of newspapers with undue force. Just as everything was getting back to where we were all reasonably happy, there went the grownups messing it all up again. I picked up the package and went around the side of the stand to deposit it on the top of the pile, which was leaning against it. In a distance I saw Uncle Henry and Father walking side by side. Father was cleanly shaved and had a new, navy-blue sweater. They were talking about something and not looking this way.

"Uncle Henry and Father are also coming to visit," I said, aware that this sort of news was bound to make an impression. Mama gave me a look as if she were lost.

"They're past Mrs. Bronski's stand and are heading this way. I just saw them from the other side," I explained.

With sudden urgency Mama grabbed Fishel by the sleeve of his windbreaker. "I'm sorry, I'm so sorry, but please, please go! Go quickly!" She was pulling Fishel away from the stand. "Theo's unpredictable; he's a bit insane. I don't know what to expect. Please forgive me! Come back tonight—or maybe better tomorrow night—when it's all over and he's gone."

She was pushing and pulling Fishel, trying to get him as far away from the stand as she could. At the same time, her eyes were searching the crowd of rushing people for Father and Uncle Henry. At the onset of her pleading, Fishel looked stunned and confused. He let himself be led and tugged and pushed. Then suddenly he grabbed his backpack and freed his sleeves from Mama's trembling hands. With the piece of paper still in his hand, he made his way up the street, taking giant strides. He didn't even look back or wave good-bye.

I still don't know what's worse: witnessing the fight between your parents or being sent away so that they may hurt each other freely without worrying about you. After sending Fishel off, Mama told me to go home. I wished I could have stayed and reminded Father about the glue and asked him if he found a job, but Mama was in no mood for arguments. Walking away, I saw her going inside the stand and closing the door behind her. Before I turned the corner, I looked back for the last time. She was sitting inside her fortifications, and Father and Uncle Henry were at the front counter, talking to her through a small sliding window. At home I tried to keep my mind occupied by spreading the pieces of the vase on the table in the big room and fitting them together. I had an idea to number them with a crayon on the inside.

Someone knocked on the door, and I went to open it. Father was standing on the stair landing, smoking a cigarette.

"May I come in?" he asked. I didn't know what to say, so I just stepped aside, and he came in and closed the door. I think there is something in the cigarette smoke that makes me cough almost as soon as I breathe it in.

"It's the smoke, isn't it? I'll go out on the landing to finish," Father said, pointing to his cigarette.

"No, no, Pa… How should I call you?" I was embarrassed.

"I'm your father. You don't have much choice," he said.

"Okay. So, you don't have to go…Papa. I'll just sit in that chair in the corner, and you'll be by the window," I said very softly. I lowered my head to avoid looking straight into his face. "You know," I continued, "there are some other kids in my class who have no fathers…but their fathers were killed in the war or disappeared, and no one knows where they are."

"I'm sorry you're not so lucky," he said.

"I didn't mean I want you to be dead or disappeared. I was just wondering if people like Fishel can get to be someone's father."

"The only way is to marry someone's mother," he said. He got up from his chair and was pacing back and forth along the table. Talking to me was making him nervous.

"But then Mama would have to get unmarried to you. If she did, what would you be then?" I asked.

"I would still be your father. I will always be your father." He stopped in front of my chair. "I'm afraid we're stuck with each other for life…you being my daughter, and I being your father. Do you mind that very much?" he asked.

"I don't know," I said. "You haven't been around long enough. Maybe if you took me to the movies… Do you like movies?"

He smiled and exhaled white smoke. "I haven't seen a movie in awhile, but I wouldn't mind going with you. We could have fun. After the movie we could go for hot cocoa and pastries." He was standing very close, and the smoke was getting to me again.

"You already promised me two things: the movie and the glue for the vase," I said trying to suppress the cough. "Do you keep your promises?"

He was looking around for something to put out his cigarette. "I always try," he said. "I'll go now. But I'll be back to take you to the movies, and I'll get the glue for your vase. You must have liked that vase very much." He made a dome out of his hands around the burning cigarette, trying to contain the smoke. At the door he turned and said, "I'll be back real soon, and before I come, I'll leave my cigarettes at Uncle Henry's."

After Fishel left us in the street so abruptly, without even saying good-bye, I was sure I'd never see him again. I felt it was Mama's fault he had stopped coming. Somehow that day at the stand she had hurt him badly. I think she knew that, and she felt guilty, but on the surface she tried to explain it away, saying he was probably busy or had gone again to Lublin. Yet it was gnawing at her all along.

Back at school it was the usual routine. Sophie was gone. Her Mama moved out to live with her sister in a small town south of the city. Mama said that Sophie would be happier living somewhere where she was not constantly reminded about her father and his death. I missed her very much. There were no kids from my class that lived close to our building, and many times during the summer, I sat by myself on the wall, swinging my legs, remembering Sophie, and feeling very lonely. At school I mostly played with Magda and Maggie Zycer, but it wasn't the same. In the afternoons I did my homework, and studied maps I checked out from our library. I was looking for Israel. It was nowhere to be found. I did not dare to ask or breathe a word of this to anyone. I didn't want this search for Israel to get out of hand like the map of America thing had. Whenever I had some time to myself, I pored over the maps of places near and far, climates warm and cold, but so far found nothing. I was beginning to doubt the place existed. One day in mid September, I checked out a book on Southern Asia. There were maps of different regions on every other page. I studied them one after another in search of Israel until I fell asleep on the South China page. What woke me up, I think, was the sound of the door being closed. I knew there was someone in the room with me.

"Who's this?" I said.

"It's me," he said, and I thought I recognized Fishel's voice.

"Is that you, Fishel? It's so dark in here. Turn on the lights. I fell asleep." The lights seemed very bright. I had to cover my eyes.

"Are you sick?" asked Fishel.

"No, I don't think so. I just fell asleep looking for…"

"I brought you presents," he said, taking off his backpack and searching in it for something. "There are people I know who get packages from America. They gave me two oranges." From his backpack he took out something wrapped in a newspaper filled with strange pictures. "These are called 'comics,'" he said, pointing to the crumpled page.

I picked up the paper. It was filled with a row upon row of small squares. Within each square there was a tiny picture. There were cowboys on horseback or holding guns and two beautiful blond girls wearing tall boots and cowboy hats. There was also an Indian who had a feather in his hair, but his hands were tied in the back. They all had bubbles with letters coming out of their mouths.

"The pictures tell a story," said Fishel. "Maybe later we'll try to figure out what the story is about. Here are the oranges." He held out two round fruits the size of large apples. I took one to examine it up close. So far I have only seen pictures of oranges but never the real things. The one I held in my hand was orange, and it smelled like a flower.

"Do they all smell like that?" I asked Fishel.

"Orange blossoms have a wonderful fragrance," he said. "I remember a flower shop in Lublin. It was next to Uncle David's bakery. There were miniature orange trees in large flowerpots. Tiny white blossoms smelled like tropical nights."

That's odd, I thought, *for tropical nights to smell like flowers.*

"What about days? Do tropical days have their own smell?" I asked.

"I'm sure they do," said Fishel. "Would you like me to open an orange for you? I'll make it into a lotus flower." He walked over to the other side of the table and put his backpack next to the shoebox with the pieces of the vase.

"How is the work on the vase going?" he asked.

I told him it was going nowhere. As soon as I put a few pieces together, they fell apart again because Papa still hadn't brought me the glue he had promised.

"I'm sure he has his reasons. It's probably imported and very expensive," Fishel said.

I watched him make symmetrical cuts in the supple skin of the fruit. The smell intensified, and the whole room smelled like a garden.

"Did he say anything about the glue last time you saw him?" Fishel asked, never taking his eyes away from the orange.

"He said he'll bring it soon."

"I see..." said Fishel, still concentrating on carving the orange. "And where is your mama now?"

"Where else?" I said. "At the stand. You can visit her on your way home."

"I'll stop by to say farewell. Today is the day for farewells," he said. I didn't understand what he meant but he continued. "Remember, I told you I had a baby cousin who was lost in the war? Well, the Red Cross people found her, and I wrote her a letter…" The orange was ready, beautifully unfolded like an exotic flower. Fishel held it out to me, but I didn't care about it any longer.

"So that's what it is!" I cried. "You are leaving too! You're going to Israel! That's why you said it's the day for farewells, and that's why you brought the oranges." I turned away so he wouldn't see me cry.

"Aggie…" he said, and he put his hand on my shoulder.

"Don't." I brushed it off. "I thought you said people should stick together because loneliness is the greatest enemy." He set the orange down on the table and put his arms around me.

"Come on, Aggie," he said. "You know if I stick around it will make your father an even angrier and more lonely man and your mother more uncomfortable with the choices she'll be forced to make. And you…what choices have you got? Either a criminal or a Jew for a father. You might be better off without one."

A dark, irreversible, and debilitating sadness settled upon me. It was futile, the wish and the effort, to keep together people torn asunder by their wills, as well as by circumstance. I was sobbing, and Fishel held me in his arms and rocked me gently as if I were a fussy baby who does not yet understand the ways life plots itself.

"I have another present for you. A real farewell present. Not just an orange," Fishel said softly. He let go of me and reached for his backpack. I was determined not to be easily won over, but receiving two presents on a day that wasn't even my patron saint's day was highly unusual.

"What is it?" I asked with my back still turned toward Fishel to emphasize my disinterest.

"It's a very old book," he said, "from long before the war. I came across it at the flea market and thought of you. It has pictures of Chinese porcelain—"

"Chinese porcelain? You mean vases?"

"Vases, bowls, figurines. Come look. I marked the page where I found the vase that looks very much like yours," said Fishel. Now I was really interested. The book had a hard cover, upon which something used to be printed with gold letters. Almost all of the gold was rubbed off, and I couldn't decipher any letters. The pages were yellow and had red edges. They were filled with delicate, intricate drawings of oriental vessels. On the upper half of the page marked by Fishel two vases of similar shape, size, and color scheme but with different designs were standing side by side. The one on the right was identical to the one whose pieces were laid out on the table.

"I wonder if Grandma ever had the other one," I said to Fishel.

"Maybe she did, and it got broken in the war, just like this one did."

"I've tried to put mine back together—see here, I'm numbering the pieces—but everyone keeps wrecking it over and over again. Papa promised to get me the glue, but he probably won't remember," I said, feeling sorry for myself again.

"If he forgets, you'll just have to remind him again. Give a message for him to Aunt Rita, or, better yet, write him a letter about the glue, and maybe draw a vase or something..." Fishel took my chin in his hand so that I had to look him straight in the eye.

"Nothing is going to happen all by itself. You have to make it happen. Insist on it happening," he said, and from the tone of his voice I understood that what he said was important. I had never before written a letter and an idea of writing one sounded like a really grownup thing to do.

"Is it hard to write a letter to someone?" I asked Fishel.

He looked at the window curtain, which was rising and falling with the breeze. "It depends. Some letters, I suppose, are harder than others..." his voice trailed off, and he was silent for awhile. He must have been thinking of something else because his eyes had an empty, absent look. He reached again for his backpack, hesitated, then opened it again.

"Here's a letter for your mama," he said, handing me a large white envelope. "It was one of the most difficult letters I've ever had to write. All the others were much easier."

I wondered why he gave it to me if he planned to stop by the stand and see Mama on his way out.

"Tell your mama I wanted to give her this letter myself but changed my mind. Think you can do this for me?"

I took the letter and put it on the top of the pieces of the vase which were still in the shoebox.

"Will you write me a letter from Israel when you get there?" I asked.

"I don't know if I'll ever get there," he said. "It's not as easy as you might think." He closed the flaps and tightened the rope on his backpack. I turned the page of the book and found a picture of a porcelain bowl with three geishas in the garden. The geishas were playing strange instruments. One of the instruments looked like a flute. The other two I had never seen before.

"Don't you sometimes wish," I said, "that people would stop constantly doing things, moving, leaving, or going places? I wish they'd just stay put like the little people on the vase."

Fishel smiled and put on his backpack. He was about to say something when the door burst open, and Mama came in, carrying groceries in two bags made of cotton yarn that Grandma T. had crocheted for her. As soon as she laid her eyes on Fishel, she became alarmed.

"What are you doing here? I thought we agreed…" I knew this tone of her voice; Fishel was in trouble.

"He brought me presents"—I lifted up the book—"a book of vases and oranges, and he came to say good-bye." Fishel seemed helpless, his long arms falling along his thin body. "He also brought you a letter he didn't want to send from Israel," I continued.

Mama's eyes were going back and forth between Fishel and me.

"What…what is she talking about?" she finally said. Fishel reached into his pocket.

"Here," he said, "I wanted to give you back the key and… I didn't want to leave without… I gave Agnes the letter…"

"Letter?" Mama said. "Something happened at the Red Cross. Isn't it what this is all about?"

Fishel's face suddenly lit up. His body became erect as if infused with new energy. "Yes, yes…it was Mirah they found. She has her own family now, but they want me to come and live with them. They are all in Israel. I have a family in Israel. My family," he repeated, as if wanting to hear it one more time.

Mama was looking at the key and weighing it in her hand. "So, that's it," she said. "You're going there too." She was still standing where she first put the groceries down on the table with her back toward the open door. She didn't see when Papa appeared and halted at the threshold. He had a small package in his hand, which, after appraising the situation, he immediately put in his coat pocket. He didn't look at Mama or at me. His gaze was fixed on Fishel. He plunged his hands into his coat pockets and walked into the room.

"Ah…who do we have here? Surprise! Surprise!" he said.

Mama turned abruptly, and I saw a wave, like a nervous spasm, run over Fishel's face.

"Why…it's my loving wife and my war buddy, my former partner in business, but presently a partner in my marriage," Papa continued. "Marriage for three—a new business proposition!" Father was slowly moving toward the table. Mama went around it and stepped in front of Fishel. The air was thick with tension. I had trouble breathing it in. The taste of fear was in my mouth. The same taste I had when Father and Mrs. Oggler went at each other.

"Fishel was just leaving, Theo. He came by to say good-bye. Just let him pass," Mama said. The spaces between her words were enormous. They stretched into dark, dangerous recesses upon which anyone could stumble and fall. Father did not pay any attention to what she said about Fishel. He pushed her aside and came up to Fishel very, very close. Fishel stepped back and dropped his bag on the floor.

"No, no," Father said. "We'll talk a bit with that son of a bitch before he goes. I have some questions for Mr. Mayer, here. And you stay out of this." He said that to Mama, but she just kept tugging at his arm, trying to pull him away.

"Please, Theo," Mama was pleading, "some other time. We'll talk some other time. Aggie's here, and…and he was just leaving. He brought her a book." Mama reached across the table. "*Look*, he brought a book for Agnes."

As if he was waving off a stubborn fly, Father freed his arm from her grasp. His voice was getting louder.

"Just mind your own business, Janie. This is between him and me. All I want is to get this straight. When did the two of you…get cozy? It was before they took us in. Isn't it the truth?"

Fishel stepped back. Father moved still closed to him, and then he yelled directly into Fishel's face.

"You wanted me out of the way…ty…ty…skurwysynu! Have enough guts to admit you're also a snitch!"

Mama kept pulling on his arm, trying to get him away from Fishel.

"Stop it, Theo!" she was yelling. "You've gone mad! Come on, leave him alone."

Father wrestled his arm free again, repeating after her, "Mad dog! I'm a mad dog!"

I shut my eyes to not see what happened next, but I opened them right away because for the first time in this argument I heard Fishel's voice.

"This is crazy! You've gone crazy in the slammer, Theo! Are you saying I sold out? I turned you and Bert in to sleep with your wife?"

"That's it! You got it! So what did they promise you, Judas, money or passport to Israel? You Jewish scum!"

Suddenly Fishel punched Father on the side of the nose. For a moment Father seemed surprised. He touched his face as if checking if it was still there. A drop of blood was running down from his nose. He suddenly bent forward, and, like a magician, he pulled something shiny out of his sleeve. There was a click, and now it looked like he was holding a knife. Fishel grabbed a chair and raised it in front of himself. I no longer understood what was happening. I ran to Mama's side. I hid behind her, put my arms around her waist, and buried my face in her back. She tried to free herself from my grip, but I was holding her tight.

"Jeeesus! Theo!" Mama was screaming. "What are you doing? Put that down! Put it down right now! Look at you… Look at yourself! You'll go right back to the slammer!" From behind Mama's back, I saw Fishel still holding up a chair and maneuvering around the table to get closer to the front door.

"This is not war, Theo!" Fishel's voice was laud but even. "Look, no enemies here, no Krauts, no Soviets. Drop the damn knife!"

I didn't know how, but I came out from behind Mama's back. I was still holding on to her arm, but I was yelling at the top of my lungs, "Please, Papa, please! I'm scared! I'm scared!" For the first time he took his eyes off Fishel. He looked in my direction, but his stare was empty, like a dark well. He didn't see me. I was not in his eye. I knew I was not there and I was not here. I didn't exist.

"The knife, Theo! Listen to me! Throw the knife! There, on the table! Now! Theo! Now!" Mama was not screaming any more. She was just urging him in a stern and steady voice.

Father threw the knife on the table. His hands fell down and helplessly dangled like on a puppet. Fishel moved calmly and very quickly. Making no sound, he put down the chair, picked up his backpack, and left the room. We were all standing in silence. Mama's arms slowly encircled my shoulders. The wave of quiet weeping rose up in my throat.

Men, Women, Babies, and Urban Inspectors

The leaves were rapidly turning red and yellow, but the days and even the evenings were still very warm. Only occasionally a gust of cold wind from the Ural Mountains, the faraway heart of the continent, would remind us that winter was on its way. Then, the yellow leaves would flutter in their branches in fear and fall to the ground. Mrs. Oggler called it the "Golden Autumn" and swore that it used to be like this every year when she was young, before the war. For a few days after school, she let me go to the small park that bordered the churchyard. There the leaves were knee deep, and they whispered their complaints when crushed under foot.

Since Papa moved out after breaking all of our dishes I spent much time in the afternoons with Mrs. Oggler. Most of the time we chatted and sampled the cakes she faithfully baked every couple of days. She was very fond of sweets. When she was busy cleaning or baking her cakes, I did my homework in her apartment or simply played with Snowy, who was always a great companion.

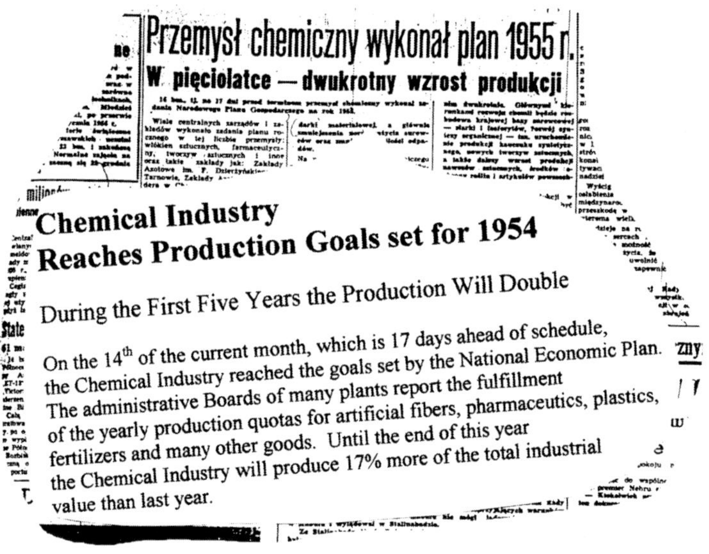

**Chemical Industry
Reaches Production Goals set for 1954**

During the First Five Years the Production Will Double

On the 14th of the current month, which is 17 days ahead of schedule, the Chemical Industry reached the goals set by the National Economic Plan. The administrative Boards of many plants report the fulfillment of the yearly production quotas for artificial fibers, pharmaceutics, plastics, fertilizers and many other goods. Until the end of this year the Chemical Industry will produce 17% more of the total industrial value than last year.

Mrs. Oggler and Mama had a pact to buy toilet paper for each other whenever one of them came across a delivery to some store in town. News of any delivery usually spread like a lightning through the neighborhood, and almost immediately a line of customers formed in front of the store. Mama's pact with Mrs.

Oggler worked so well that many times we had run short of basic things like salt or flour, but never of toilet paper. Since we had lived with a nationwide shortage of paper for as long as I could remember, store customers had to provide their own bags and paper to wrap and carry home their shopping including meat and produce. The simplest way to haul home the toilet paper booty was to string ten or twenty rolls like beads and hang the enormous toilet paper necklace around the neck. Those people who tried to use trams or buses while wearing their toilet paper necklaces became subjects of endless jokes and wisecracks. I hated traveling with Mama or Papa when one of them was wearing the toilet paper. It was so humiliating to have one of my parents, in public, a subject of vulgar and raunchy comments. I wished I could shrink and hide in one of their pockets.

Mrs. Oggler was always very good at tracking the deliveries and nailing her place in the line.

Thanks to her, our stockpiles of toilet paper were considerable. As a matter of fact, we had so much of it that Mama occasionally bartered it away to Aunt Rita for other scarce items like honey or raisins, which I adored.

Hearing a commotion on the staircase, I ran to the front door to check if, by any chance, it was the mailman. Against all odds, I was still hoping that someday I would get a letter from Israel. Instead I found Mrs. Oggler with three strands of toilet paper rolls hanging from her neck and carrying two bags full of the contraband veal cutlets. One of the toilet paper strands got caught on the doorknob of the apartment below us. I helped her up to her apartment with one of the bags. She offered me crumb cake and a glass of milk with honey. Mama never made crumb cake, and Snowy was already purring and rubbing against my leg, so I stayed a little longer chatting with Mrs. Oggler.

Mrs. Oggler's apartment was exactly like ours but clean and very nicely furnished. She even had a china cabinet and a piano in her big room.

"Do you ever play on your piano, Mrs. Oggler?" I asked while dividing the crumb cake into four small pieces so that it would last longer.

"It's been a long time," she said, "Last time I did it was during the war, when Mr. Oggler was still with us." She poured the warm milk into a tall glass. "I played waltzes for him. He liked waltzes. Would you like some more crumb cake…what is it your Mama calls you?"

"She calls me 'mouse,' but since I turned twelve, I've decided to become a larger animal," I said, and suddenly I remembered that Mama told me to stay home this particular afternoon. I was to wait for Aunt Rita who was bringing us additional coal rations for the winter. Mrs. Oggler, Mrs. W., as well as other weather specialists were predicting a very severe one. As usual, we were counting on Uncle Henry to have a few extra coal rations to keep us warm.

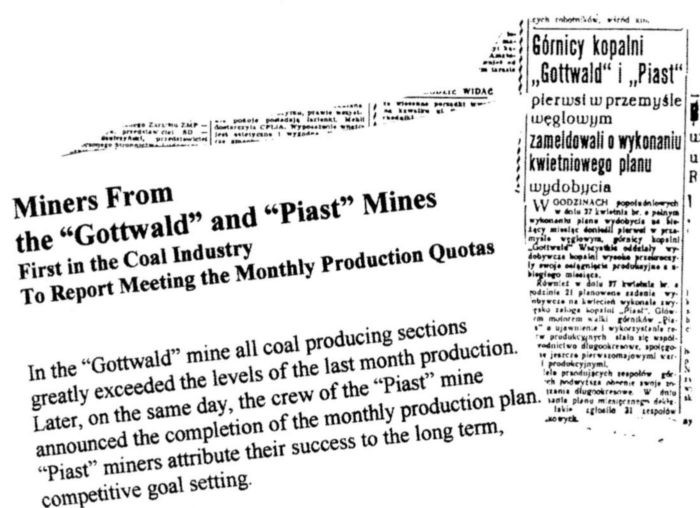

Miners From the "Gottwald" and "Piast" Mines

First in the Coal Industry To Report Meeting the Monthly Production Quotas

In the "Gottwald" mine all coal producing sections greatly exceeded the levels of the last month production. Later, on the same day, the crew of the "Piast" mine announced the completion of the monthly production plan. "Piast" miners attribute their success to the long term, competitive goal setting.

I ran down the flight of stairs separating our apartment from Mrs. Oggler's two steps at the time. Aunt Rita arrived a few minutes later. She was tired and not at all in a good mood. While I was fumbling around with the teakettle, fixing the tea she had asked for, Aunt Rita took off her shoes, nestled in the old stuffed chair, and said, "I think I'm pregnant. You know what that means, don't you?"

I was too embarrassed to admit how little I knew, so I nodded and said nothing. I pretended to busy myself pouring more sugar into the sugar bowl and washing off teaspoons.

"Both Henry and I, we are not the kind of people who should have children. We are much too selfish…and times are too uncertain. What would we do with the baby?" she continued. Then realizing that I might not be quite ready to be drawn into a grownup girl's talk, she added, looking thoughtfully at me, "Your Mama did talk to you about…you know…men, women… and babies?"

"Yeah…sort of…" I said.

"What do you mean 'sort of'? She either did or didn't." Aunt Rita was indignant.

"Well… she was sort of busy…and…"

There was a loud knocking at the door, and for the time being I was saved. I wasn't about to freely admit that all I knew about "men, women, and babies" was what I either overheard or learned from my friends. I also remembered when I came upon Uncle Henry and Aunt Rita in their car. By then, I figured out that making babies required taking off underwear and somehow connecting the private parts of the two people involved. But even though this thought was immensely disgusting, the subject of baby making remained utterly fascinating. After seeing Uncle Henry and Aunt Rita the most solid source of information on the subject proved to be an old marriage manual from before the war, which had been circulated sometime ago among the girls in our class. Unfortunately, the book was confiscated by Mrs. Pawlak when she caught Magda Zaycer reading it during the grammar quiz. This incident was followed by many lengthy and heated discussions among our trio (Magda, Maggie, and I) as to the mechanics of the sexual act itself, but since we were lacking the original text to support our various arguments, our discussions usually led nowhere. I felt that whoever was now knocking at our door had, indeed, saved me from appearing very childish.

"Who is it?" I asked.

"Urban Inspectors. We want to ask you a few questions," said a man's voice from the other side.

I looked back at Aunt Rita. She was getting up from her chair. Just a minute ago she had seemed relaxed and in a reflective mood. Now, all of a sudden, her face became very tense and serious.

"Just a moment," she said loudly, and she hurriedly started to put her shoes back on. Without a word she motioned me to open the door.

At the first glance, the man at the threshold seemed familiar. He was tall and bald and wore a long leather jacket. He smiled at me as if he knew me. But when he looked into the room and saw Aunt Rita, his face became solemn. Behind him on the landing were two other men wearing trench coats and hats. They all looked odd because the weather was much too warm for their heavy, autumn garb. The urban inspector looked at the paper he was holding in his hand.

"Do you know one Mar...Marta Pien...Pienko?" he read slowly. "Is this her apartment?" He directed the question to no one in particular, so I felt obligated to answer.

"I don't know anyone by that name," I said. "No one by that name lives here."

But the inspector was not satisfied.

"We know she lives in this building. The question is in which apartment. She's a tall, big woman. Wears a black coat. Her hair is up, braided on the top of her head—" he was saying when Aunt Rita interrupted:

"My niece said we know of no one..."

"But that's Mrs. Oggler, Aunt Rita! Mrs. Oggler looks like that!" I cried, all excited because I was able to solve the puzzle ahead of everyone. "She lives right above us, one flight up," I added. Aunt Rita's hand came to rest on my shoulder and squeezed it very tightly.

"Excuse us, please," she said slowly. Her voice was much louder than usual. "My niece is very sick. Don't pay any attention to this foolish talk. She's been feverish all morning. We're waiting for the doctor. He should be here any minute." She was leading me away from the door.

I looked at her, bewildered.

The urban inspector was no longer interested in us. He turned to his companions.

"You heard the girl. Let's go," he said.

Aunt Rita closed the door slowly, and then she leaned her head against it. Through the door came the sound of heavy footsteps going to the upper floor.

"Aunt Rita," I asked, "did I say something I shouldn't have?"

We forgot to turn on the lights. When Mama opened the front door, the room was already filled with dark, blue shadows. I was sitting close to Aunt Rita. She was holding my hand. We had been talking about men, women, babies, and urban inspectors. Such topics are much easier to talk about in the dark. By now I pretty well understood how things were between men and women and babies, I mean, where the babies came from. With urban inspectors, it was a lot more difficult.

Mama turned on the light and suspiciously looked at Aunt Rita and me.

"She had a lesson about human biology and then another one about morality and ethics," said Aunt Rita, stretching in her chair and almost knocking over her tea, which had already gotten cold. "We had no trouble with the biology. Your daughter was more than ready for that part. It's the morality that's still a little problematic."

I was expecting Mama to ask questions about the "biology" part, but she acted as if it was perfectly normal, which greatly surprised me. She even seemed sort of relieved. Instead, she asked Aunt Rita about Father. Since the day he had pulled the knife, I hardly ever thought about him. Fear was an unpleasant memory. Mama had never shown any interest in what was happening to him either. I thought she was afraid of him too. I looked at her for a long time, trying to determine what had changed, why she was all of a sudden concerned about his fate. Her mood had shifted, I felt that, but I couldn't precisely say how or why.

"The news is good," said Aunt Rita. "He's working."

According to Aunt Rita, Pan Przemek, whose last name was Wysocki, was a "dirty, old bachelor." He took Father in for old time's sake and was able, through his connections, to find him a job. So, Father became an inventory clerk at the spare parts warehouse, which belonged to the Public Bus Transportation. Pan Przemek, Aunt Rita said, was also "relatively dry" because, some time ago, his liver and kidneys refused to cooperate, so he did not drink as much as he used to.

"Of course, at least a quarter or more of Theo's pay probably goes back to his boss in the form of English whiskey and American cigarettes," laughed Aunt Rita. "Other than that, he's doing okay. He paid Henry back the money he had borrowed in July, and since then I've never seen him drunk. He's staying off the sauce."

I was watching Mama. She was chopping carrots and rinsing sauerkraut, but she was also listening very intently. It was good to hear that Father had a real job and that he was, in the words of Aunt Rita, "staying off the sauce." I remembered him standing with a teakettle and saying how afraid he was that Mama would leave him. And then another picture of him stalking Fishel with a knife was there, under the surface. These conflicting images of him, the mixed feelings I had about him, the visit of the urban inspectors, the sudden burden of Aunt Rita's revelations, all of this was altogether too much. Suddenly I burst into tears as if some dam inside me had given way.

For Mama and Aunt Rita, my howling and tears came out of the blue. They both tried to comfort me, but Mama, probably suspecting that my fit of crying had something to do with talking about Father, attempted to distract me. Changing the subject, she asked, "Where did you put the coal rations from Aunt Rita?"

Still sobbing, I pointed to the drawer where she kept extra house keys, recipes, and old electricity bills. She hugged me again and said, "Looks like you had a rough day, Mouse. Did you go at all upstairs to visit Mrs. Oggler?"

"She already has company," said Aunt Rita, lowering her voice to a whisper. "A few thugs from the secret police. They're still there, probably going through her stuff. They came looking for her some hours ago."

Mama's face turned pale. She sat down right where she was, at the kitchen table, and kept stubbornly looking down at the space between her feet.

"They pick them off like flies, one after another…" she said. "And why? What for? For trying to survive as best they can…?" She raised her head. Tears were streaming down her face.

"I don't blame Theo anymore," she said. "What I'm doing at the stand is more or less the same thing. Small cunning deals, dirty little lies, to cheat them and survive. I'm slowly chipping away at my honesty, and it's eating me alive. If Theo and Marta are guilty, so am I. I should be next on their list."

Later that evening after Aunt Rita had left, Mama was still very upset about Mrs. Oggler. She paced up and down the room, looking helplessly at the ceiling from time to time. The building we lived in dated back to a time well before the war. Mr. Galazka, our janitor, said it was a solid house because it survived two plagues, the Nazis, and the Soviets. The rooms in our building were tall, and the walls were thick. We couldn't hear what went on upstairs. We couldn't even hear footsteps. While Mama paced back and forth, I was sitting at the table in the big room, turning the pages of Fishel's book of Chinese porcelain. I was looking at the pictures but not seeing them at all. I think I was as upset as Mama. In my head, Mama's words about being guilty and next on the list to be arrested were stubbornly ringing. I was unbearably afraid of losing her too. Too many people had disappeared from my life lately. It no longer mattered whether they went to prison or somewhere else. The aftermath was the same—their sudden absence and then the emptiness they left behind. Going to prison, I found out, did not necessarily mean that someone did something bad or was a bad person. More than anything, it seemed to be a question of strange coincidence.

Outside it was completely dark, and almost all the windows in the building across the street were rectangles of yellow light drawn upon the blackness of the night. Mama stopped her vigil and went to the kitchen to make us something to eat. While she was there, I let Fishel's book fall in my lap. I held my breath and listened to the sounds she made in the kitchen. I wanted to hear her knocking pots, chopping, or running water in the sink.

"Come on over, Mouse, and set the table for the two of us," she called. "The sauerkraut broth and sausage are almost ready. Are you very hungry?"

"Not very, and not for sausage," I answered. "Don't you think that since I'm almost thirteen, I could become a larger animal than a mouse?"

She looked me over and smiled. "You're too skinny for a rhinoceros."

"Oh, quit kidding me," I said, offended. "How about a kitten instead of a mouse?"

"I'm sure that could be arranged. So what were you up to all day, my kitten?" she said.

"I had crumb cake at Mrs. Oggler's, then a grownup talk with Aunt Rita, and just now I was looking at the picture of Father's vase in the book Fishel gave me. Do you think he will write me from Israel?"

I remembered the letter he wrote to Mama and left with me. The one I put in the shoebox with the pieces of the vase on that awful day when Father went mad. That evening, after Fishel and Father had left and the water for tea was boiling, I gave the letter to Mama. It must have been very sad because she cried all the time while reading it.

"I want to get a letter by real mail, and with a real stamp," I said, "but I don't want to cry like you."

"I'm sure Fishel will write you a happy letter. Israel is a happier place. Oranges grow in Israel," Mama said.

Why can't we go to Israel? I thought. Mama could run her newspaper stand without the "little lies" and without the "cunning deals," Fishel could visit us, and…

"Do you think Father would be very mad if we went to Israel too? Would he try to cut us up with his knife?" I asked.

For some reason Mama suddenly got mad at me. She slammed the cover back on the potato pot and said sharply, "Oh, stop talking nonsense, Aggie! You know he didn't mean to cut anybody up. He just got upset. After being where he was, people get touchy."

I looked at her, surprised. I remembered her fear as well as I remembered mine. Why was she lying to me now? "It still makes me afraid of him," I insisted. "I wish we could go to Israel, at least for a little while."

"To leave here and go to Israel, you have to have family there and be a Jew," Mama said, and I detected a note of irritation in her voice.

"What is it about Jews?" I said. "First they're unlucky and get killed and lost in the war, and then they get lucky and can go to Israel when no one else can. Are they different from everybody else?"

"No, they're not," Mama said, spooning potatoes on our plates. "It's just that we sometimes make them out to be. When it's convenient. Here's the plate with the sausage."

We sat down and started our supper in silence—Mama eating slowly and probably thinking of Mrs. Oggler, her newspaper stand, or maybe Father, and I, afraid to interrupt, waiting for her to look at me or to say something. I realized that if we were to stay like this, just the two of us (Fishel gone to Israel and Father, God knows where), this was how it was going to be—very quiet. I didn't like the quiet. It was lonely. "Loneliness is the greatest enemy," I remembered Fishel telling me once a long time ago. In the silence hanging above our kitchen table, the knocking on the front door came very loudly. In a way I thought it came right when I wished it would. I jumped from my chair and was the first to the door.

"Who is it?" I asked.

"It's me…Theo…your papa… I brought you the glue." Papa wasn't exactly who I had wished for at that very moment. I was a bit alarmed, having him right outside the door. Back at the table, Mama was already eating her broth. I grabbed her arm and was frantically tugging on it.

"It's Papa! He brought me the glue! What do we do? Do we open the door and let him in?" I was so agitated that I managed to spill some of the broth from her spoon onto the front of my sweater.

Mama answered me also in a whisper, "Of course we do! Calm down, for heaven's sake! Don't be afraid. Your papa loves you. That's why he's here. Wipe that stuff off your sweater, and let's open the door." She handed me a dishrag. "Now, go on. Open the door."

I went back to the door very slowly. This was how it happened:

I opened the door and stepped aside. There was an uncomfortable moment of silence. I knew Papa was hesitating, because I was watching his shoes and they were not moving. Mama came into the hallway from the kitchen and said, "Well…come in, Theo… and close the door. The evenings are already cool and the apartment is barely warm from the heat of cooking."

Papa stepped in, and I closed the door behind him. We both walked into the kitchen and stood there side by side. Mama looked at us and laughed.

"Don't just stand there with your heads down like two convicts. Take your jacket off, Theo. Put it on your bed, Aggie." She then told Papa one of those things that were neither the truth nor a lie.

"We were just talking about you. Aggie was going to write you a letter…isn't that right, kitten?"

I didn't remember when I had told her about Fishel's suggestion that I should write a message to Papa reminding him of the glue, but I must have, because otherwise, how would she know? In the meantime Papa took off his jacket and handed me a small package wrapped in red tissue.

"They were decorating the warehouse for the anniversary of the October Revolution. There was a lot of that stuff lying around," he said and pointed to the red tissue. "The glue is inside." I felt a small bottle through the thin layer of paper.

"Oh, Theo! You didn't have to do that, you know," Mama said. "Especially now, when you have no money. I know how expensive things are when they're imported."

"It's no big deal. The vase…it was my fault. Aggie liked that vase so much. I really felt guilty." He turned to me. "What were you going to write in your letter?"

I felt like I was not thirteen or even twelve. I felt like I was a small child questioned by an adult just to pass the time. What he asked and what I answered him had no bearing on anything and was of no importance. I was so embarrassed by this game that I was unable to raise my eyes and look at him. What I really would like to know was when he pulled the knife, did he mean to use it, or was it just to scare Fishel? And why was Mama suddenly so nice to him—only because now he had a regular job, like she had wanted, or did she want him back because Fishel was not around anymore? But children cannot ask adults questions of this sort, and I was afraid to be the cause of a flare up, in the aftermath of which I might lose one of them or both. I needed to answer him before this silence became awkward.

"I was going to write about the glue," I said, "a real letter…and I was going to draw the vase, just the way it was before. There's a picture of it in this book… it's a book of Chinese porcelain…"

I think the book of Chinese porcelain was not a safe territory and that was why Mama interrupted. "We were having supper. Sit down, have some soup with us, Theo," she said. "I still think you should have been more sensible than run out and buy this glue. Aggie, please get another spoon for your papa."

When I brought him the spoon he turned around and said, "If you want, I can help you with the vase after supper?" He was sitting at the table and looking up at me in such a way that I could not avoid his gaze any longer. "Please, let me help you," he said very softly.

I looked at Mama for her permission to agree, but there was energetic knocking on our front door. Mama turned in her seat towards the door and whispered, "This place is as busy as the central station at peak hours," and to the door she said loudly, "Yes?"

"This is the urban inspector. I have a message from your neighbor." His voice was low and the tone very decisive.

Mama and Papa rose in their seats. I rushed to open the door. One of the men wearing a trench coat and hat stood on the landing. He was holding the same canvas bag Mrs. Oggler used to carry her contraband veal cutlets.

"Your neighbor upstairs asked to give this to Agnes," he said. "You're Agnes?"

I nodded and he handed me the bag. Just then Mama came to the door.

"The neighbor upstairs?" she repeated after the Urban Inspector. "Do you mean Mrs. Oggler?" The man hesitated for a moment, but Mama was very impatient. "What's going on? What's happening to Mrs. Oggler?"

The man ignored Mama's questions and started to go, but before vanishing into the darkness of the stairwell he turned around.

"She has to come with us, maybe even stay for awhile. Good evening to you," he said.

I closed the door in a hurry. I was curious what was in the bag, but Mama and Papa were acting strange. They just stood there for a long while, silently looking at each other. Then I remembered what Aunt Rita had told me and what the man in the trench coat had said. It all probably meant that Mrs. Oggler was also going to prison. I understood that in a small, incidental way I had played my part in it. Aunt Rita said it was beyond my control; she said I should not feel guilty. Still, in a way I felt I was, and I delayed looking into Mrs. Oggler's bag. Out of it came a small, white, furry paw trying to catch my finger and play with it. It was Snowy! She meowed, jumped out of the bag, and with her tail straight up in the air paraded around the room as if she owned the place.

Princess Dragonfly

It was a Sunday, last week in September. The doorbell rang, and Uncle Bert and my cousin Bella were at the door. I could still remember her wearing a tight, berry-colored coat and holding fast to her father's hand. Mama looked at them and instantly knew something was not right.

"What's with Ola?" Mama asked. Aunt Ola, which was short for Aleksandra, was Bella's mother. She had a strange illness that no one dared to name.

"She had to go in again," answered Uncle Bert. "The doctor says this time it is going to be a long while." What this meant was that Bella would be staying with us until her mama came back from wherever it was she had to go. I was so happy, I felt like grabbing Bella and dancing around the room. But dancing was not such a great idea when everyone had a long face, including Bella.

Other people went to the hospital when they got very sick, but Aunt Ola went to a different place, which was called a sanatorium. When people said the word *sanatorium*, they usually lowered their voices and put on the look of knowing sadness, which was like saying, "We know it is hopeless, and we're sorry."

In the encyclopedia, the definition of a sanatorium did not sound half as bad: "institution for rest and recuperation" or "establishment for the treatment of the chronically ill." After looking up *chronically*, I knew Aunt Ola had an unnamed and incurable disease. When I finally asked Mama what was wrong with Aunt Ola, she said that Aunt Ola's nerves were acting up again. It was then that I started to suspect Aunt Ola was crazy. *Nerves* was a code word for that.

A couple of days later, I looked at the newspaper Mama brought home from the stand. There was an article in it about a lunatic asylum and a doctor who was locked up in it not because he was crazy, like Aunt Ola, but because he refused to talk. It seemed that the lunatic asylum and the sanatorium were two completely different things, even though people who were crazy could end up in both places. From what the paper said, the first was more like a prison. Of course, I didn't tell any of this to Bella. All the reading and looking up I had done was for her. She wanted to know what was wrong with her mother, but no one would tell her.

Bella didn't talk much or ask many questions. Sometimes we made a deal, and I asked the questions for her. It used to be that Mama sent me to stay with Bella for two or three weeks every summer. Bella and her folks lived in a small town about fifty kilometers from the city. My visit to Bella's house was always the highlight of the summer, which otherwise I usually spent at home. Her household was wonderfully weird, and Bella and I had practically unlimited freedom to do what we pleased, with plenty of open spaces to do it. I remembered Aunt Ola never wearing any street clothes and never leaving the house. She usually wandered around in a long, flannel nightgown and flowery robe with lace ruffle at the sleeves. Her hair was long, half black and half gray, and always a mess. She didn't talk much to anybody but softly sung odd tunes, mostly to herself. I think Bella got to be so quiet because she could never really talk to her mama. Bella was a great friend once you got used to her silent ways. Aunt Ola never asked where we were going or what time we'd be back. Come to think of it, she was never interested in anything but singing, watering plants, and looking through old, yellowed sheets of music. All was well with her until last summer. Since then, Aunt Ola had been in and out of the sanatorium, and Bella had grown even quieter than before. Sometimes the two of us could have an entire conversation with me doing all the talking and Bella just nodding or turning her head, pointing with her finger or rolling her eyes.

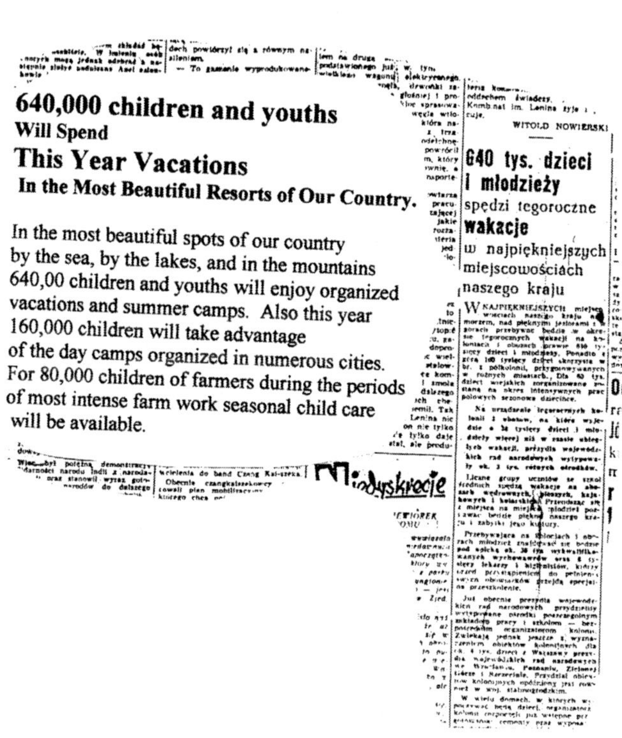

640,000 children and youths
Will Spend
This Year Vacations
In the Most Beautiful Resorts of Our Country.

In the most beautiful spots of our country
by the sea, by the lakes, and in the mountains
640,00 children and youths will enjoy organized
vacations and summer camps. Also this year
160,000 children will take advantage
of the day camps organized in numerous cities.
For 80,000 children of farmers during the periods
of most intense farm work seasonal child care
will be available.

Last summer Mama put a small black suitcase and me on the bus that stopped almost in front of Bella's house. Bella's house was on the outskirts off a small town named Konin, right next to the main road. A couple hundred meters farther, the road narrowed and went over a small bridge. From then on meadows spread out on both sides of it. There were no more buildings or any other structures in sight, only small grassy hills and an occasional cow or a flock of dirty sheep. What was flowing under the bridge could hardly be called a river. It was a stream of water about three meters across at its widest parts. The bottom was sandy with a few larger boulders protruding here and there from the streambed. Reeds, tall grasses, buttercups, clovers, and forget-me-nots grew in abundance along the banks.

Bella and I would start our day under that bridge. We would leave our shoes hidden in the grass, hitch up our skirts, and slowly move up stream, inventing and playing games as we went. Flies were buzzing, dragonflies skimmed the stream surface, sun danced on the ripples—we were lost in the magical world where nothing evil could touch us. A dragonfly momentarily rested on Bella's forehead, a rainbow glimmered on its wings, and suddenly Bella became Princess Dragonfly, my daughter. I was the dragonfly queen. We wove crowns of grass, lupine, and buttercups for each other. We were on a quest to recover the Emerald Wing, which Princess Dragonfly lost from her crown. We were followed by a string of attendants; the reeds were the footmen, the grasses curtsying maidens. Our golden path meandered, and we had to overcome various hurdles like deep wells (where the water was deep enough to get our panties wet) or devil's gates (wooden footbridges too low for us to pass under). The sun was high and the air was very hot. We had been wading in the stream for a good two hours or maybe even more. Around another bend, we came up against a tall, stone wall. The stream flowed from underneath it through a stone pipe, which was very wide. As a matter of fact, it was wide enough for us to crawl through, perhaps getting our bellies only slightly wet. We had never gone this far up stream before. I climbed out and sat on the bank. Bella followed. The wall was old, crumbling, and there were some stones missing at the very top. I lifted Bella to get a look at what was beyond the wall. Was it worth crawling through the pipe? When Bella got down, it was my turn, but she could hold me up only long enough for one glimpse. What was beyond the wall looked like a park—dark, shady, old, and leafy trees of all kinds. From a distance, I caught a glimpse of birch trees because of their white bark. Next to the wall Bella found chestnuts still encased in their prickly green shells, looking like porcupines.

"This is the ultimate test, dear princess," I said. "If we crawl through that pipe, we are sure to find the Emerald Wing."

Bella was so enchanted that she forgot she was Bella and began to talk. "But, Your Motherly Highness," she said, "what if the wicked gnome lets the water out of his bucket and drowns us when we're crawling through the pipe?"

"We can't be drowned, silly. The pipe is too short. We just hold our breath and go through."

"Okay, maybe," said the Princess, "but then what do we do on the other side? What if there is someone real and we get in real trouble?"

"Then I'll say that it's my fault because I'm older, and I made you come with me. Let's go, my dear princess. It'll be all right," and we hitched up our skirts again and crawled into the pipe on all fours.

We emerged on the other side and looked around. Signs that in the past this used to be someone's enormous garden were everywhere. An unpleasant moment in the slimy darkness inside the pipe was well worth it.

"It's like having our own secret garden," said Bella. We both recently read the book. We scurried around, tracing the pebbled paths, which used to run between low hedges. We stopped by rose trees gone wild and shapeless but still in bloom, marveled at pink morning glories, which once upon a time had been confined to winding up the graceful stone arches over the paths. Now they were cascading like waterfalls from the old trees.

Not too far from the wall next to our stream, we spotted a ruin of what looked like a stone gazebo. This definitely qualified as a romantic ruin. We climbed two cracked steps leading up to the platform where there were broken stone sections of what once might have been a column. Everything was overgrown with ivy. A large, brown toad presided over the ruin. It watched us while we disturbed its peace and trampled the vegetation. Suddenly Bella shrieked with excitement.

I quickly put my hand over her mouth. She pulled me over to show me another, larger "romantic ruin" farther in the distance beyond the trees. This ruin looked like a manor. It no longer had a roof, but the wall facing us was pretty well preserved. In the middle of it there was a large opening flanked by columns—three on each side. Farther to the left of the last column the wall was beginning to crumble and it ended in a heap of plaster pieces, broken bricks, and cement chunks. The right side of the wall had fared better. Three dark openings marked locations of where the windows used to be. We didn't need to discuss strategy any longer. Once Bella decided to do something, she was in all the way. We broke into a sprint to see who would get there first, but after the first few steps, I knew I was going to lose this one. Bella was light as a dragonfly and just as swift. Her feet, from running barefoot all summer, had soles thick and tough as leather. I was a city girl with delicate feet, no match for Princess Dragonfly. Bella waved to me from a distance and disappeared between the columns.

The closer to the ruin, the better and wider was the path. I tried to pick up my pace, but strange things had been happening to me lately. I had gone through a growing spurt this summer, which made me almost as tall as Mama, but I felt very awk-ward in this larger, heavier body. It was as if my legs and arms belonged to two different people, and my head to still another one. I tripped over my own foot, which was at the end of the leg that had become too long; I fell and skinned my knee. Limping and jumping the rest of the way, I rushed into the dark mouth of the ruined building.

Something struck my back and pushed me into the ground. Then my head was being covered with a thick blanket. I was fighting for breath, and struggling to throw off the weight that was holding me down.

I heard a coarse voice bellowing right over my head. "Lie still, I tell ye! Lie still, ye, gypsy bitch!"

I realized the voice was talking to me. I was the "gypsy bitch." I stopped struggling and felt the weight that was pressing upon me being partially lifted. I also felt my hands being tied behind my back.

"Git up, and keep yeer spells to yerself. I got me holy cross hanging on me neck, so yer spells ain't worth a wart! Do what I tell ye and no darn magic or devils." He pulled me up to my feet by the shirt on my back but left the blanket on my head. Then he led me somewhere in the dark. After a couple dozen steps, he pushed me into what felt like a small enclosure. From the sounds that followed, I guessed that someone else was also being hauled into the same place. I heard the door being closed and bolted. I figured it was the door leading to the place I was in.

As soon as the footsteps of the man died down, I softly called out Bella's name. Sure enough, she was there next to me. Her hands were also tied, but she didn't have a blanket over her head. I crouched next to her, and she grabbed it and pulled it down. He must have thought I was more of a threat.

Bella showed me how scared she was and that she didn't struggle at all when he grabbed her, and how he wound the rope around her hands and feet. We were locked in a small, wooden shed. There were cracks between the boards and some boards were rotten. We took turns looking outside through the biggest crack, which was as high from the ground as Bella's knee. The shadows were growing longer, and we figured that it was already past our dinnertime. Usually we would show up at home when Uncle Bert came from work at the furniture plant. He brought the groceries and fixed our meals because Aunt Ola always left things unfinished and went on to doing something else. We figured he should start worrying about us right about now. Time passed and I heard the sound of an engine coming closer and closer. The engine stopped somewhere very near. Through the crack, I saw a young militiaman and a large old man limping in front of him and pointing to the shed.

"You better have a good reason, Matthew, for dragging me away from the dinner table," said the militiaman.

"Yes, yes, very good, sir! I've got me two gypsies, the old mother bitch and a gypsy bastard. Them two been poking around, looking to steal something, throw spells on innocent believers…"

"There's nothing here to steal, Matthew," laughed the militiaman.

"What about them apples and strawberries that belong to the collective farm? And my pipe tobacco? They was after my pipe tobacco."

"Well…where are they? Let me see them." The young man was impatient.

I looked at Bella and then at myself. We did look like gypsies. Our hands, knees, and calves were brown and green and caked with mud from crawling through the muddy pipe. Some of the mud had also gotten on our clothes and faces. We had wilted grass and flowers in our hair, and we were barefoot. But above all we were tanned and our hair was naturally dark and curly. The door to the shed opened, and the head of the young militiaman appeared.

"Come on closer, the two of you," he said. I was determined to speak up and explain the situation, but he took one look at Bella and said, "Aren't you the daughter of Bert Korsak?"

Bella nodded her head.

"How did you get so far from town? Cut these ropes, Matthew," he ordered the old man.

"We walked along the stream," I volunteered, massaging my wrists where the rope left marks on the skin.

"And who are you?" he looked me over quickly.

"I'm her cousin."

"What we have here, Matthew," said the young man, "are two girls who lost their way in the fields. Next time you better mind your apples, your strawberries, and your liquor."

"It's one of 'em evil spells! I swear on my soul they was gypsies when I got 'em!"

The young militiaman looked suspiciously at the old gardener. "You didn't do them any harm, you old billy goat?"

The old man stepped back and crossed himself.

"Come on, girls, I'll give you a ride home. Have you ever been on a motorcycle?"

We followed him obediently beyond the row of jasmine bushes where he parked his dusty machine equipped with a sidecar. I climbed in first, and then Bella sat between my legs. The wind was warm, and Bella's hair was flying all over my face. At breathtaking speed, we passed fields, meadows, and birch groves that were nothing but a blur. When we came close to our small bridge and the first buildings of Konin, the motorcycle slowed down. From the bridge, the house where Bella lived was in plain view.

There was an ambulance parked in front and a few people gaping at the building entrance. We stopped at the curb, and while Bella and I were clambering out of the sidecar, the militiaman jumped off his bike and came up to two men who were standing apart from the rest. They were close enough so that we could hear what they were saying.

"What's going on here?"

"It's the Korsak woman. They've come to get her again," said the stocky dark haired man. "This time she's locked herself in the bathroom. She's been there for hours."

"Maybe she's already dead—cut her wrists or something," said the other.

"Shhh! I just brought her daughter back home…" The militiaman looked back in our direction. By the time I understood what was being said, Bella was running home. I followed her, unsure if it was what I should be doing. The building was a long, one-story rectangle occupied by two families, one at each end. In the main hallway, however, there was one bathroom both families had to share. In front of the bathroom door several people had gathered. There was Uncle Bert pale, shaky, and very distraught, all the neighbors from across the hall, and the ones from across the street. There was also a young doctor, two medics, and an ambulance driver. The ambulance driver was holding an axe. He was about to break down the bathroom door. The hallway was not very well lit. The light bulb over the bathroom door cast a semicircle of yellow light. Bella stopped just outside of the ring where she could not be seen. I was one step behind her. She knew I was there right next to her. She grabbed and held my hand.

The driver took a few swings at the lock then pushed the door with his shoulder. The breaking wood was creaking and moaning. It was a frightening sound that found its way deep into the very center of my body. The door flung open, and I saw Aunt Ola folded up and squeezed into the corner behind the toilet. It was hard to comprehend how she could have fit herself in there. Her eyes were wild with fear. She screamed, bit, and fought the two medics, who were trying to pull her out from her hiding corner.

I had never seen Aunt Ola like this. It made me very uneasy, maybe even scared. But I looked around and all the neighbors were quite calm, just curiously looking at her and the medics. Bella turned away and buried her face in my armpit. She made no sound, but her body was wracked from time to time by a nervous spasm. Her nails dug deep into my skin. All I could do was to put my free arm around her and hold her. When it looked like the medics were succeeding in prying Aunt Ola from behind the toilet and pulling her away, she suddenly grabbed onto the pipe that ran between the toilet and the water tank high up there, almost under the ceiling. Both the tank and the pipe came off the wall, crashing down on Aunt Ola and the two medics. One of them was hit on the head and stunned. All were wet, including Aunt Ola. But she was momentarily free. She stood straight, very proud of what she had done; and then she strolled out of the bathroom, stepping gracefully over the debris, lifting the hem of her robe. The neighbors made way, and she walked on, out of the building and toward the back of the ambulance where the doors were wide open. Without looking back, she climbed in and closed the doors behind her. Everyone was so still the silence hurt inside my head.

Maggots

Magda Zaycer was doing a report on socialist revolution in China. I told her that my book of Chinese porcelain didn't have any of that stuff, but she wanted to see it all the same. Mama didn't want me to bring strangers into our house, especially when she was not there, and all my friends from school, Mama said, were strangers to her. She said our house was horrid, and it looked like a gypsy camp because no one took care of it, and there was no money to buy any furniture. I made Magda promise me that she would wait in the hallway while I got the book.

The book was usually on the windowsill, next to the vase, which was already half-way done. Papa told me that what we had been doing to the vase was called reconstruction. It meant putting something back together using the same materials it was built with in the first place. But you had to add something new, something to hold the pieces together. And that was the glue, which he had brought. On my way out, I noticed Papa's black suitcase, the one he had taken with him when he was moving out. It was standing in the middle of the table.

I really didn't feel like lending the porcelain book to Magda Zycer and letting it out of my hands, but Papa's black bag on the table in the big room was distracting me. I wanted to get back in there and check it out before anyone else arrived home. I let Magda take my book. After I closed the door behind her, I rushed to the big room and opened the bag. There was no doubt it really was Papa's bag—Fishel's sweater, which he had taken when he was leaving, was right on top. Now it looked like he had moved back in again.

Funny, just a few days ago it seemed, I thought Mama and me, we'd be lonely, and now we already had two extra people, Papa and Bella, living with us. I wished Bella were back from school so that I could tell her about Papa moving back in.

Mama had enrolled Bella in the fifth grade, but Bella was behind in Russian and she had to take classes after school to catch up. Poor Bella! She was not too keen about talking, and here she had to do it in still another language. The doorbell rang—we had a doorbell now since Papa started coming to help me with the vase and fixed the wire, which was disconnected—and I let Bella in. Behind her was this dark, shabbily dressed fellow with a large, leather pouch resting on his belly. He said he had a telegram for Mama, but he needed her to sign for it. I didn't remember that we had ever received a telegram. I was very curious how it looked, whom it was from, and what it said, but the telegram messenger—that's who he said he was—refused to leave it with me. He wanted Mama and that was it. I sent him off to Mama's newspaper stand and went to the kitchen where Bella was making sandwiches of bread and butter sprinkled with sugar.

While we ate, we speculated about the telegram and about Papa moving back with us.

"Maybe he is just going to keep his bag here," said Bella. But this didn't seem right.

A big, noisy fly was buzzing around the kitchen, trying to land on a square of butter. It was late in the year for the flies to be out and about. Usually at this time they were snuggled up somewhere for the winter. But this fall felt like Mrs. Oggler's "golden autumn" from before the war, and even the flies were confused. Here we were in the middle of October, and we still were running around without sweaters or jackets. Everything with Papa became clear when we heard the key opening the front door and he let himself in. He was carrying a load of white sausage for dinner. I quickly looked in the junk drawer where Mama kept coal rations, old electric bills, and the house key, which Fishel had returned before leaving for Israel. The key was missing.

Before he got arrested, Papa was never interested in what was happening in the kitchen, as long as the food that came from there ended up on his table and plate. Now I looked at him surprised. He was wearing Mama's flowery apron and was chopping onions. The stove was fired up and the oven was hot. He was going to bake the sausage smothered in onions. About an hour later, Bella and I were sitting on the windowsill, counting the streetlights that were coming on one by one. Some of them flickered in the blue air as if they were winking our way. I saw Mama turning the corner into our street. She was walking very fast, almost running. When she came in, all out of breath, Papa was trying to show off his dinner of baked sausage, potatoes, and pickles. He was very proud of himself, but Mama was upset over something. She ate very little and did not pay him much attention. Bella and I, on the other hand, gorged ourselves on the sausage. White sausage was rarely at the state-run meat stores. I was finishing the second helping of the sausage when Mama got a yellow folded sheet of paper out of her bag. I guessed that it must be the telegram. Without a word she put it on the table in front of Papa.

"May I look at it too?" I asked.

"Later. Now you and Bella clean off the table," said Mama, and I knew we better be quick about it.

Once we got the dishes into the kitchen and left Mama and Papa in the big room, we slowed down. We played with the water in the sink while talking about boys in general, and a certain Pawel who followed Bella home from school, tossing pebbles in her direction. The big, brown fly was out, sampling the leftover sausage.

It was very quiet in the big room. Mama was curled up in the stuffed chair. Papa was standing by the window with his back to the room. His hands were stuck in the pockets of his pants. He was looking at the darkness outside. The telegram had been abandoned. It was sitting like a large, yellow butterfly in the middle of the empty table among the crumbs of mashed potatoes and pieces of onion.

"May I look at it now? I asked again.

"Go ahead," said Mama as if she cared neither about the telegram nor anything else.

The yellow paper was lined like a school notebook. Between the lines, pieces of paper tape were pasted. On the tape words were printed with what looked like faded black ink, all in upper case. This was what it said:

MOTHER HAD STROKE STOP OUT OF DANGER
NOW STOP NEEDS EXTRA CARE STOP COME
IMMEDIATELY STOP PIOTR

Piotr was Mama's brother who lived in a small village at the edge of the forest. He worked for the Department of Forestry. Grandma T. lived with him. Grandma T. was Mama's mother.

"If you're still thinking of bailing out of family life, this is the time to do it," said Mama. Papa didn't answer. While he continued to watch the darkness through the window, I wanted to question Mama about the telegram, but she was in no mood.

"Take Bella and both of you do homework in the small room," she said impatiently.

Mama said that misfortune liked company. When it came you could always count on more of it to follow. I supposed she meant Mrs. Oggler, Aunt Ola, and then Grandma T. I really felt sorry for Mama. When I looked at her tired and irritated all the time I wanted to hug her and hold her tight, but she was so cross with everyone and so tense that in the end I decided to stay out of her way. I knew I should also feel sorry for Grandma T., but Grandma T. was a difficult person to like and her misfortune turned out to be very lucky for Bella and me. Because of her misfortune we got to travel on the train. Mama was fixing cheese sandwiches for the trip.

Bella was excited and also a bit afraid. She had never been on the train before. The sandwiches were supposed to be with the leftover white sausage, but there were little white worms crawling all over the sausage and the plate. Mama was going to send me out to the basement where there were garbage cans for the whole building to use, to get rid of the sausage, but Papa had a weird idea, to which Mama said, "Now, that's disgusting, Theo," but he went ahead and did it anyway. He said he knew of only one place in the city where you could buy fishing bait. He found the information in the paper because the authorities were making a big deal out of it. When he went there a few weeks earlier with Pan Przemek the place was boarded up and no one knew when it will be opened again. He said we would be better off raising our own bait.

So now on the windowsill in the kitchen we had a glass jar covered with a piece of thick paper and secured with blue string. Inside the jar were the leftover sausage and the maggots. That's what the little, white worms were called. Papa said all they needed was air and sausage, and they would double in size overnight. Bella and I had made tiny holes with Mama's needle in the paper covering the jar. Papa said maggots made great fishing bait, and that there was a small lake near where Uncle Piotr and Grandma T. lived.

"While you and Piotr slug it out who's to do what about the 'drill sergeant,' the girls and I, we're gonna do a little fishing. Hear that, girls?" said Papa.

I was trying really hard to feel sorry that the "drill sergeant," which was Grandma T., was sick. But this misfortune was turning out to be a lot of fun.

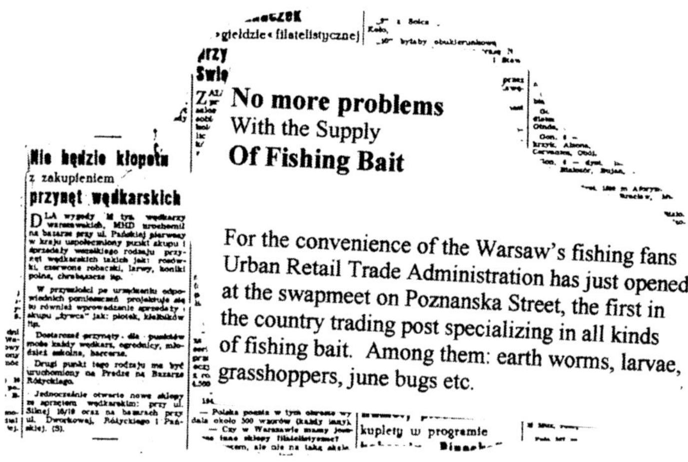

We didn't have many pieces of luggage, since we were only going there for two days, and Papa's black bag would suffice. The next important thing was the bag with food and then Papa's fishing gear. He had to find his fishing rods, rubber boots, and tackle box. All that stuff hadn't been out of the cellar since the summer before he got arrested. Bella and I helped him with his tackle box. Inside we found his old fishing cap and many things we didn't know what to do with.

"Gosh, you need all kinds of stuff to catch fish. It looks a lot more complicated than I thought," I said. "So many things to do before you even cast a line."

"I promise to teach you everything I know about fishing," Papa said, "but still it might not help us catch any."

We cleaned the box and arranged the hooks, the lines, the floats, and the weights. Papa put his old fishing cap on.

"I'm sorry I didn't burn this thing when I had a chance," Mama said, pointing to the cap. To tell the truth, it did look kind of ugly.

When the tackle box was all ready and organized, Papa put the jar with the wriggling maggots on the top and closed the box securely. Mama didn't want anything to do with the tackle box since she knew the jar with the maggots was in it. She said that raising maggots for bait and transporting them flew in the face of all rules of hygiene. She swore that if we caught any fish, she would not touch it.

We were waiting for Uncle Henry to take us to the station in his car and to bring Aunt Rita here. She was going to stay at our place, feed Snowy, and take care of the newspapers at the stand. We were leaving late in the evening and would spend the night on the train. To pass the time waiting for Uncle Henry, I brought out a map and asked Papa to show Bella and me the way the train would travel and the place we would be getting off. It was an old map printed before the war. I found it at the bottom of the wardrobe where Mama kept stuff that belonged to Grandma Aniela.

"We'll go west," said Papa. "On the map, it is to the left."

We traced thin, red lines, which marked railroad tracks. Most cities we would be passing through had two names on this map. Papa said it was because when the map was printed, the Germans thought this part of the country would belong to them. On the map it looked like we would be very close to Germany. The place where Grandma T. lived with Uncle Piotr was closer to Berlin than to where we lived. It was a small dot on the map with a small blue spot next to it. The blue spot was the lake where we would go fishing. The name of the small dot was Mysliborz. Under the name there was no German translation. "Maybe the Germans were only after the big cities and didn't want any small villages," suggested Bella, but to me that did not seem like a sound plan.

We got to the train station long before the train was due to arrive.

"Why do we have to wait so long?" asked Bella, who was getting very sleepy. The big clock above the platform showed eleven fifteen. I promised myself to stay up until after midnight. The train was due to leave in half an hour, and Mama said it should be rolling in any time now. Over the last fifteen minutes, the platform had become very crowded. People with bags, baskets, and simple bundles made out of tarpaulin or blankets were milling around, waiting like us for the train. Just then I noticed that Papa had disappeared. Suddenly a low murmur rose from the crowd, and it began to move.

"The train is rolling in," said Mama. "Let's stay behind this pole while everyone else makes a run for the passenger cars."

"Where is Papa? Will he find us?" I was worried he would be lost and we would have to leave him behind.

"He went ahead to where the train was parked on the side tracks to get a separate compartment, just for us," Mama said.

"Can you do that?"

"You can do many things that don't seem possible, if you have the money," said Mama. I guessed Papa must have paid someone to get the separate compartment. We clung to our luggage and to the pole while Mama stepped up on the tackle box to see above the crowd.

"Who are you waving to?" Bella asked her.

"It's Papa. He's two cars down, in the third window. Let's keep together." Mama pushed her way through the crowd, carrying the black bag in front of her. Bella and I followed with the rest of the gear.

Papa leaned through the window, and Mama handed him our entire luggage, and then she lifted Bella. Papa grabbed her, and before she knew what was happening, she was inside the compartment. I was already too big for that sort of thing. Together with Mama, we made our way through the crowd to the car entrance and squeezed along the corridor to our compartment. The *Reserved* sign was posted on the door, but through the glass I saw Bella by the window and Papa already reading his paper. I wondered how much extra money it took to have the *Reserved* sign posted on the door of your compartment. Mama knocked on the glass, and Papa pushed the door aside to let us in. From the crowd of people in the corridor, a young man stuck his head in the door.

"Could you spare a seat for my wife? She's pregnant," he said.

"All right," Papa said, "where is your young mother to be?" People stepped aside to make room for the woman, who did not look much older than I. Her hair was cut very short and was almost white blonde. She moved slowly through the corridor packed tightly with people, trying to protect her belly from the crowd. Once in the compartment, she collapsed on the seat next to the door and closed her eyes. I examined her face closely – she was very pretty –and then I calculated that last June she must have still been in high school and either graduated or quit to get married. Now she had a husband to cook for, and laundry to do, and pretty soon she would have a screaming baby to take care of. And that baby would be with her for years and years to come… There was a sharp jolt, and the train slowly began to move along the platform. Bella and I jumped to the window.

When I opened my eyes, the lights in the compartment were out except for the little green light bulb over the door. I was curled up on the seat with my head on Papa's lap. He was snoring away, sitting up in the corner. Bella was sleeping on the seat across from me with her head on Mama's lap. The train rocked steadily, plowing through the immovable darkness that enveloped the world outside and us on the train. I wondered what time it was.

Suddenly there was a crashing noise, prolonged scream of the brakes, people falling and crying everywhere. Papa and I flew off our seat and landed on the one across, on top of Bella, Mama, and the pregnant girl. The train came to a halt in the middle of nowhere.

Uncovered -
West German and American Intelligence Operations Against Poland

As we have previously reported within the territory of West Germany there are numerous centers of Secret Intelligence gathering. Those centers operate against the interests of Poland and other countries of the Peace Camp. They are managed and financed by the monopolistic elite of the USA. The following facts confirm the close cooperation of the American and neo - Nazi intelligence in their war mongering and anti -Polish maneuvers.

"What the…heck?" said Papa climbing to his feet. "Is everyone okay? Some drunk must have pulled the emergency brake." Bella was a bit frightened, and Mama had to explain to her what had happened and what an emergency brake was. The black bag with our things had fallen down from the luggage bin, which was over the door. All our shoes, jackets, and Mama's purse were on the floor or under the seats. Papa opened the window, and we looked outside into the solid blackness. Along the train the men from the railroad crew were walking with flashlights, carefully looking under the cars and in the bushes beside the tracks.

"Looks fishy," Papa said closing the window. "There're too many jackasses in plain clothes among the railroad crew."

Mama's eyes widened, and she turned her head toward the pregnant girl, who was in her corner and looked sound asleep.

The lights on the train were still out, so for the next half an hour, we sat in the darkness, parked in the middle of a dark field. Finally we started moving but never got up to real speed before we rolled into a small station. The signs said, "Gorzow Wielkopolski."

Except for the pregnant girl who remained asleep, we all crowded next to the window. The station was lit with fluorescent lamps, but at each end of the platform, there were additional very strong lights mounted on top of military cars. They flooded the platform with white light, which made everything look like in the movies. There must have been fog out there in the fields, beyond the station, because wisps of it were drifting across the tops of the tall fluorescent lamps. The platform was swarming with soldiers whose faces and uniforms looked waxy and silvery white in this light.

"What's going on, Papa?" I asked.

"Darn if I know. It looks like special units to me." He lowered his voice. "State Internal Security, which explains the plainclothes jackasses."

The soldiers ran, forming a line along the train and then a ring around each car entrance. When the train came to a stop, they boarded each car from both ends and squeezed through the crowded corridors and compartments, shining flashlights into passengers' faces, looking under the seats and in the luggage bins. Papa opened our door. The crowd in the corridor was very quiet. Occasionally someone coughed, but no one was talking.

Two soldiers entered our compartment. One more remained in the doorway. The flashlight illuminated Mama, Bella, then stopped on the face of the pregnant girl, who in this white light suddenly looked like a boy to me. She rose, and the light pointed to her big belly. She stepped aside, and the soldier with the flashlight checked the space under her seat. In the meantime the other soldier was checking our luggage bin.

"You've got something crawling around here," he said, "Can't tell what it is, but it's some bugs for sure."

"Oh my God, Theo, it's the maggots!" cried Mama.

"What?" said the soldier, who was still fumbling with the flashlight up there in the luggage bin.

"Maggots," said Papa. "You know, for fishing bait."

"How disgusting!" said the other soldier. "Let's get out of here." Just then the lights on the train came on, and I saw a few maggots squirming on the floor of the compartment. Two or three were exploring the seats. Mama covered up her mouth as if she was going to throw up and squeezed into the small space next to the window. She was trying to get as far as possible from the luggage bin. Papa climbed up there, and the hunt for maggots began. He squashed them with his shoe and wiped them off with pages of his newspaper. Bella and I took on the ones that had somehow made their way down from the bin. We giggled and thought it was really funny. The entire army looking on a bunch of people squashing wriggling maggots! We began to horse around, jumping over the seats and crawling under them. Even Mama got into the act and occasionally smashed a maggot that Bella and I had missed with the flat side of her purse. The soldiers standing outside the window of our compartment were smiling.

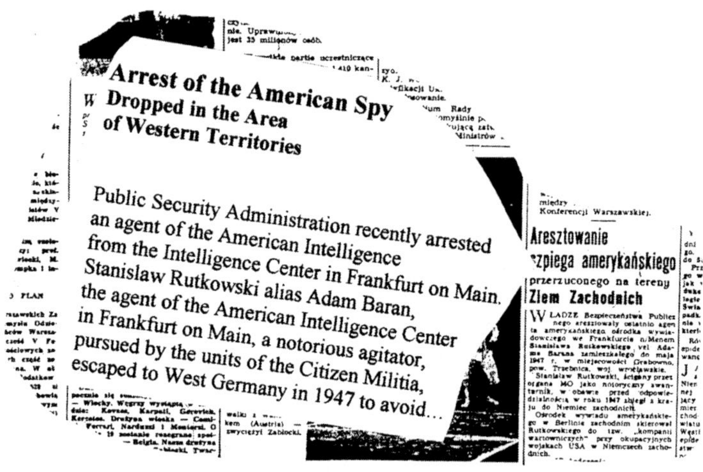

Arrest of the American Spy Dropped in the Area of Western Territories

Public Security Administration recently arrested an agent of the American Intelligence from the Intelligence Center in Frankfurt on Main. Stanislaw Rutkowski alias Adam Baran, the agent of the American Intelligence Center in Frankfurt on Main, a notorious agitator, pursued by the units of the Citizen Militia, escaped to West Germany in 1947 to avoid...

Just as Papa finally came down from the luggage bin, the train began to move again. I looked around and noticed that the pregnant girl was gone, but since no one else was paying attention, I had no time to think about it now. Papa was carefully holding his cap in both hands. In it was the maggot jar with the sausage.

"The paper must have somehow been punctured when the train was braking," he explained. "You want to give me a hand and hold these?" He pretended to give Mama the cap with the jar and the rest of the maggots. Mama squealed and jumped back. We all laughed, and then Papa motioned with his head toward the window. The train was picking up speed. The row of soldiers' faces and uniforms shinning white in the fluorescent light was quickly becoming a blur. Mama pulled down the window and Papa flung the cap with its load.

"Maggots to maggots…" he said.

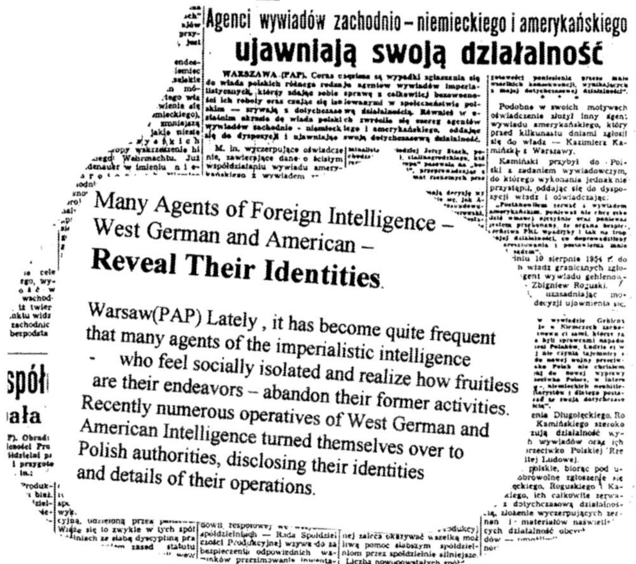

Many Agents of Foreign Intelligence – West German and American –
Reveal Their Identities.

Warsaw(PAP) Lately , it has become quite frequent that many agents of the imperialistic intelligence – who feel socially isolated and realize how fruitless are their endeavors – abandon their former activities. Recently numerous operatives of West German and American Intelligence turned themselves over to Polish authorities, disclosing their identities and details of their operations.

Walking on Ice

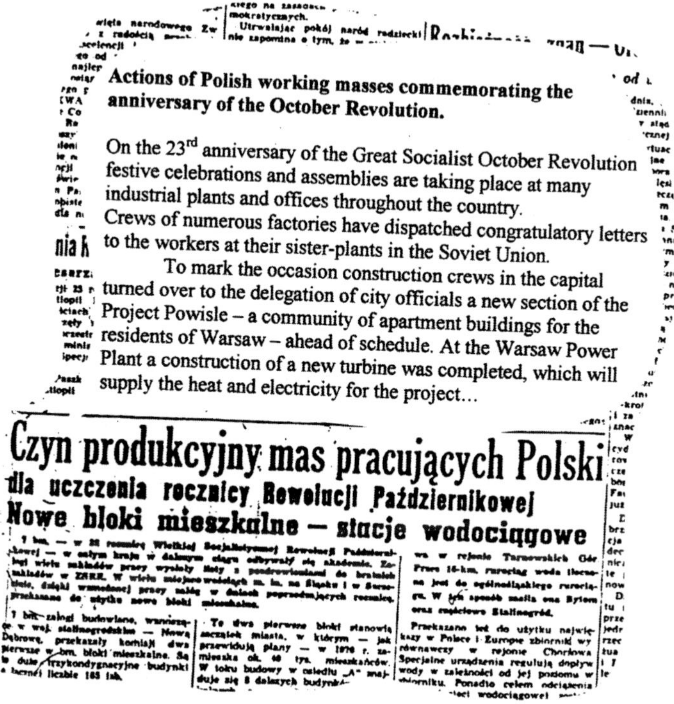

Actions of Polish working masses commemorating the anniversary of the October Revolution.

On the 23rd anniversary of the Great Socialist October Revolution festive celebrations and assemblies are taking place at many industrial plants and offices throughout the country. Crews of numerous factories have dispatched congratulatory letters to the workers at their sister-plants in the Soviet Union.

To mark the occasion construction crews in the capital turned over to the delegation of city officials a new section of the Project Powisle – a community of apartment buildings for the residents of Warsaw – ahead of schedule. At the Warsaw Power Plant a construction of a new turbine was completed, which will supply the heat and electricity for the project...

Winter came very suddenly that year. The second Monday in November, we woke up to frost glittering on the blades of grass and on the thin fingers of young maples under our windows.

"Mark my words," Grandma T. said to my mother, "it's going to be a nasty one. I can feel it in my bones." Mama went about her business not minding Grandma T.'s prophesies much at all. Lately Grandma T. felt so many things in her bones that her "feeling in the bones" lost most of its credibility.

"How do you feel winter in your bones, Grandma?" asked Bella.

"It feels as if they were covered over with a layer of ice."

"But what happens to the bones under the ice?" Bella persisted.

"They go to sleep," said Grandma T. "Deep, cold sleep."

Next morning, Bella and I were busy trying to break with sticks the layer of ice on the water in the gutter. Bella insisted she wanted to wake up the water from a deep, cold sleep. Over night the temperature dropped about ten degrees to minus-fifteen degrees Celsius, and the ice in the gutter became so thick we broke our sticks and gave up on waking up the water.

Grandma T.'s meteorological predictions and a sudden drop of temperature had their effect on my mother. In the evening she put a bowl of pickle soup in front of Papa and said, "Agnes needs a winter coat. Her old one was already tight under arms and around the chest last season. This year it will go to Bella."

I was very proud of growing, especially around the chest, which still appeared very flat in comparison with, let's say, Aunt Rita's well developed bosom. But my father continued eating his soup without as much as glancing away from his plate and at my promisingly expanding chest. Instead he carefully contemplated bits of dill floating in the yellow, round eyes of fat.

"If she needs a coat," he finally said, "go ahead and get her one. There's nothing to debate."

He didn't seem interested in the mechanics of purchasing children's winter coats. But mother offered the information anyway: "There's nothing to be bought at the state stores, as usual. I'll probably end up going to the swap meet after payday. I saw beautiful sheepskin coats on the Zycer twins last Tuesday. Zosia Zycer said they were smuggled in from Bulgaria and that Mark knows someone…"

Papa pushed away his bowl and leaned back in his chair. "I know for a fact," he said, "that Mark Zycer joined the party. Janek

Gorko, the guy that sells American cigarettes to me, also works at the Central Dairy plant. He says Zycer has lately become very popular with his bosses. Last month he got the bonus for exceeding production norms, and there is talk around the plant that he is getting a new apartment before Christmas. You don't get new apartments just for having fair eyes!"

Mama stopped loading potato pancakes onto a large blue dish.

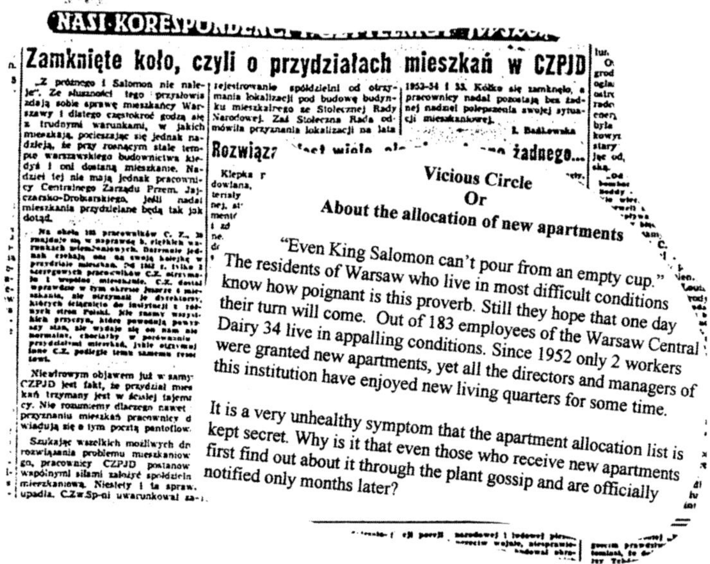

Vicious Circle
Or
About the allocation of new apartments

"Even King Salomon can't pour from an empty cup." The residents of Warsaw who live in most difficult conditions know how poignant is this proverb. Still they hope that one day their turn will come. Out of 183 employees of the Warsaw Central Dairy 34 live in appalling conditions. Since 1952 only 2 workers were granted new apartments, yet all the directors and managers of this institution have enjoyed new living quarters for some time.

It is a very unhealthy symptom that the apartment allocation list is kept secret. Why is it that even those who receive new apartments first find out about it through the plant gossip and are officially notified only months later?

"So what d'you want me to do? Stop talking to Zosia Zycer just because she has a stupid husband?" Zosia Zycer was mother's friend from before the war. They went to school together or something. Papa knew that too and wanted to avoid the fight.

"All I meant to do was to warn you. Watch what you say when you're with her. You never know what may come of it."

Silence descended upon the kitchen, but Mama was mad. I could tell she was mad by the way she shoved the blue dish onto the table and slammed the cupboard door after getting the salt and pepper shakers.

As Grandma T. predicted, after that first night the world went into a deep freeze. Day after day, the temperature hovered around minus-twenty-five degrees Celsius.

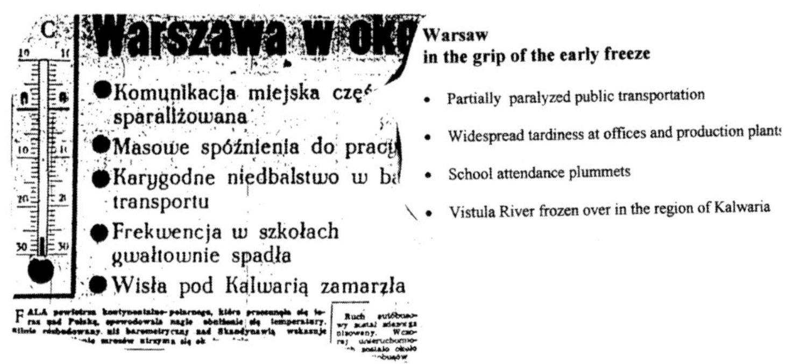

Bella and I, having one warm coat between us, mostly spent our time indoors, except for walking to and from school. We traded the coat from day to day and on the days Bella had the coat, I wore a light parka with so many layers of clothing underneath that the small swelling on my chest was totally undistinguishable and my arms stuck out strangely to the sides. In the afternoon we read stories to each other or played cards on the windowsill until it was completely dark. The world outside appeared in various shades of gray, brown, and black, but it was most of all dirty. There was no trace of snow. Trees were bare and almost black. Even the bark of the silver-skinned maples seemed to be darker this winter, almost steel blue. Blades of grass, brownish-black, stood frozen like porcupine needles, and branches of the jasmine bush, which reached the window, crumbled in our fingers. Grandma T. went on to predict that the snow would not come until Christmas, and in the meantime, the freeze would surely kill all the seeds, and there would be no crops, that all the trees will die, and even the rose bushes cowering under the straw skirts would perish in this freeze.

"Your mother is becoming a fulltime prophet," Papa said to Mama about Grandma T. "She surely is generous when she's miserable, sharing it with everyone."

Before Grandma T. came to live with us and took up half of the small room, Mama used to bring daily newspapers from her stand every evening. I got into the habit of reading at least two or three stories just to find out what strange things were happening to people all the time. But Grandma T. changed all that. On her very first morning in our house, she sent me out to get the paper for her, even before I left for school. That morning I was late for my math class. Since then I was getting the papers for her every day. Grandma T. spent her mornings reading them and marking the places she wanted me to read aloud after I came home from school. I hated those reading sessions, not only because the stuff she had me read was terribly boring but also because I was missing out on the precious playtime. Since in the afternoon Papa was usually at work and Mama was selling newspapers at the stand, I had to argue my point with Grandma T. by myself.

"Why do I have to read that stuff?" I asked her one afternoon.

"Because it's nothing but lies," she said.

I looked at her in disbelief. "Why would you want to listen to lies if you know they are lies, Grandma?"

"Because unless you know how lies sound, you cannot tell them from the sound of truth. I want you to learn how to do this, how to tell a lie when you hear one, or when you read one."

"Can you do that?" I was in awe. I wished I could have the same kind of power, simply to be able to tell if Magda Zaycer was telling the truth about kissing the new boy in the cloakroom.

"You have to practice every day," said Grandma T. "And pretty soon you'll be able to find the tiny grain of truth upon which every great lie is built. Then you can discard the rest and just keep that tiny grain."

"Okay," I said. "Where do you want me to start, Grandma?" She pointed me to the article on the first page of the *Zycie*

Warszawy—this was the very page I usually skipped because it was exceedingly boring. Now, as I was reading aloud about the "celebrations by working masses commemorating the anniversary of the October Revolution" and paying close attention to what I read, I realized that it appeared boring because I did not know anybody who could qualify as "working masses." I also knew no one who celebrated the "October Revolution." When I asked Grandma T. who would be "working masses" and if we knew any, she explained that people who worked like Mama and Papa and Pan Janek Gorko (who worked at the Central Dairy) and Uncle Bert were not working masses but individual people working to make a living. She said that "working masses" was just an empty word that pretended to have a meaning but really didn't.

The individual working people did not celebrate "October Revolution" on their own. At work they were forced to celebrate by their party bosses. I knew how that worked because at school we also celebrated October Revolution instead of a math test, and that worked out real well. So here we had another word, *celebrate*, which pretended to mean something else than it really did. I also knew from school what October Revolution was, but Grandma T. said, "Why would you want to celebrate somebody else's revolution? A Soviet Revolution?" By then she was all worked up and continued, "We have our own revolutions, uprisings, battles and such to celebrate. October Revolution and all its celebrations are just an opportunity to spread more propaganda. No one in their right mind believes this communist garbage!" And although she had already lost me with the "propaganda" and "communist garbage," she hooked me with the fishing for words that were suspect. And this was the end of my first lesson.

This was really about the river and how I had come upon it for the first time in winter, and how it enchanted me. We lived about two kilometers away from it. On our bank the land was flat, so a large dike was built to protect this part of town from flooding. In the spring, the river came all the way up the dike. The water was the color of coffee with milk, and the current was very swift. It carried bushes, tree trunks, branches, and other debris.

One spring I remember seeing a table floating upside down, half submerged, with its legs sticking up. I also remember a cow, moving swiftly downstream with its head raised high, bellowing sadly into the air. Grandma T. was there with me when I saw the cow. She lied to me, seeing how agitated I became. She said that its owner was waiting with a net and a rope downstream to rescue the animal. I knew right then she was lying. And it was all for nothing because I kept hearing in my head the animal's desperate mooing for many nights after that. Grandma T. never took me down to the river again. I think she was then already afraid of dying, and she wanted to keep this fear at bay, even if it was just the cow's death, not her own.

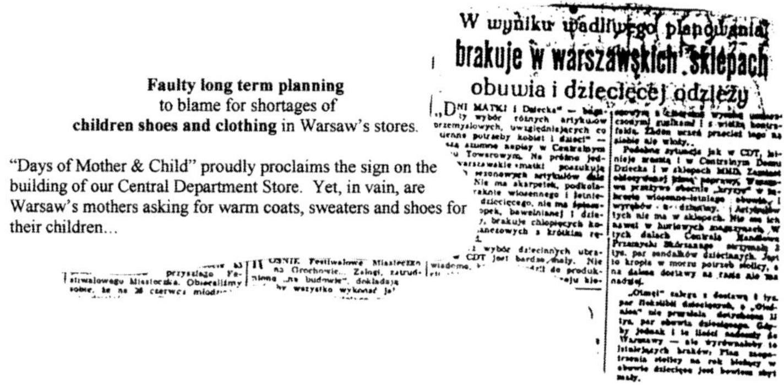

Faulty long term planning to blame for shortages of **children shoes and clothing in Warsaw's stores.**

"Days of Mother & Child" proudly proclaims the sign on the building of our Central Department Store. Yet, in vain, are Warsaw's mothers asking for warm coats, sweaters and shoes for their children...

I saw the river in winter for the first time when Mama took me to the swap meet to get the coat. It was Thursday in late November. Thursday was a market day. On that day Mama took us out of school early and left Bella home with Grandma T. so that I could have the one coat we had between us for the trip. We boarded the tram number twenty-four, which was to take us across the river to the part of town where the swap meet was held every other Thursday. Mama was tense and impatient on such occasions.

"Hurry up, Agnes! Button up! The later we get there, the more crowded the place will be, and crawling with pickpockets and other human scum." She was constantly afraid of being robbed, and to be doubly safe she put a wad of bills destined to finance my coat into her brassiere. I saw her doing that and was mortified in advance, imagining the scene at the swap meet when she would try to get the money out to pay for the coat and one of her enormous breasts would slip out of its harness and into the public view. I continuously thought about it from the moment we left the apartment, boarded the tram, up until the tram entered the bridge. It was an old, narrow bridge. Two lanes of traffic going in opposite directions were separated by two sets of tram rails. Upon entering the bridge, tram number twenty-four slowed down to a snail's pace until it reached the middle, and there it stopped altogether. All passengers patiently waited for the tram to resume its course, but nothing happened.

People started talking to one another in hushed voices. Some tried to ask the machinist why the tram suddenly stopped, but he didn't know either.

I was getting bored standing next to Mama, breathing in the stale odor of clothing, sweat, and mothballs. I even forgot about the fat roll of money snugly nestled in her bosom. A couple, evidently in a hurry, rose from their seats and got off the tram, intending to cross the rest of the bridge on foot. Mama pushed me to the window seat and heavily sat beside me.

Below the bridge, as far as I could see, was a field of glittering whiteness. The river was frozen over, and it was a magical sight. *How could the dirty, murky water freeze into such beauty?* I wondered. The surface was uneven, and small mounds of ice threw purple shadows onto the surrounding whiteness. Here and there the whiteness was so intense that in the sun it became turquoise and even pink. But most of all it was the vast expanse of purity, something untouched and unsoiled, that attracted me. I pulled myself up onto my knees on the wooden seat and pressed my face against the glass. I knew I would have to go there and see this miracle up close, witness it directly, first hand, and not from the distance. I turned away from the enchanted river and set back quietly in my seat, trying hard to conceal my inner excitement.

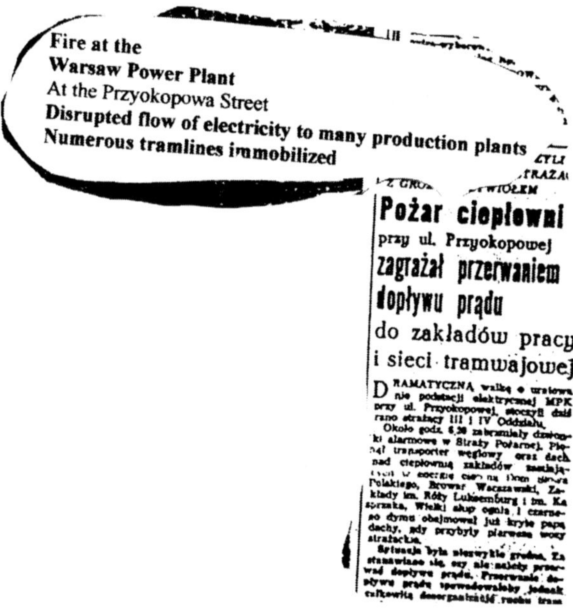

Steadily more and more people were walking on the bridge in the direction where our tram and the other trams had come from. I saw three men approaching our tram. One of them was in a uniform of the People's Militia. The other two wore plain clothes. The militiaman accompanied by one of the plain-clothed fellows climbed onto the front platform where the machinist was seated. The other man stood outside, watching our tram. After a short, hushed exchange with the machinist, the militiaman addressed the passengers: "Comrades and citizens, we ask you to leave the tram and go back to the last tram stop. The bridge has been closed and will remain closed indefinitely.

There has been an explosion at the Warsaw Power Plant headquarters, and the tram rails have been damaged. We suspect sabotage by the enemies of socialism and other counter-revolutionary elements."

"What does 'counter-revolutionary elements' mean?" I whispered to Mama.

"It means we won't be going to the swap meet."

I finally got my new coat about three weeks later. The freeze was still holding the world in its grip. Bella and I were already thoroughly disgusted with the one-coat situation. The Christmas break approaching, we were looking at the prospect of snow, everybody playing out during the day, and the two of us with one coat to share. It was downright depressing. We talked about it at length, sitting perched on the windowsill, looking out at the dirty world. Coat or no coat, we were desperately praying for snow.

Papa came home from work bringing with him Pan Janek Gorko, the man who sold him American cigarettes. I didn't like Pan Janek right from the start. His nose was very large and red with a purple tip. I don't know why it made me think of a certain poisonous mushroom whose name I quite forgot. After he and Papa had a few shots of vodka—to help the circulation—Pan Janek's eyes became narrow slits in his spongy face, and his voice turned to coarse whisper. He brought a package wrapped in the newspaper, which he presented to Mama. It turned out to be Papa's favorite white sausage, a delicacy not to be easily obtained in the state meat stores.

After dinner, when father and Pan Janek were already smoking and on their second bottle of vodka, Mother summoned me to the big room, which also served at such occasions as a dining room.

"Agnes, come here, young lady. Father wants Pan Janek to take a good look at you, how big you've grown."

The slits in Pan Janek's face became even smaller when he tried to focus. He beckoned me closer with his finger and told me to turn around. I stepped forward and smelled the sour odor of his breath. He kept shaking his head.

"I don't know… I don't know… She really is a big girl. How old…how old did you say? Twelve? Almost thirteen…" He looked at me, concentrating mainly on my chest. "I will have…to measure," he muttered under his breath.

Mother left the room to fetch a measuring tape, but Pan Janek had another type of measuring in mind. He spread his wide, hairy paw from my armpit across my right breast and, pressing hard, counted off, "One." Then he proceeded to place it on my left breast, thoroughly mashing it with a middle of his palm, and counted off, "Two." I had an urge to draw back from Pan Janek's heavy paws. There was something slimy and unclean in his gestures, an urgency and strange hunger I've never experienced before. In agony and confusion, I sought Papa's eyes. But his gaze was fixed on the glass, which he was filling with vodka, and then on the ashes balancing on the tip of his cigarette. In a way he was like Grandma T. that day on the river. He was avoiding something because of fear. Quietly, without one glance, he also corrupted me into silence. From among us only the cow, desperately mooing and knowingly paddling to its own death, was the honest creature.

I turned out to be two of Pan Janek's paws across the front and one and a half across the back. The measuring session was concluded just as Mama came back with the tape. She put it on the table, but Papa waved her off, saying Pan Janek didn't need it any more. She looked at him and wrinkled her forehead then shrugged her shoulders and left the room.

Next day father brought home my new coat. It was a Bulgarian sheepskin, warm and light as baby's breath. Its only fault was, in Mama's opinion, that it was bright green. Birch leaves when they first open in the spring have this greenness, which later hovers over the tree like cloud and catches the eye.

I loved my green coat. It was a bit long, and we had to roll up the sleeves. It was, however, perfect around the chest. Mother said that because it was double breasted, each year, as I grew, we could move the buttons and adjust it to my size. Father was obviously pleased with himself. I felt that in some strange way it had to do with Mark Zycer having to join the party to buy his twin girls sheepskin coats, and Father being able to manage it without such an ultimate betrayal. Mama was proud of him too. "In the end," she said to me, "it turned out right that we didn't make it to the swap meet that day. I know you were disappointed, Aggie, but God has a way of making things turn out right." I somehow could not reconcile God's intervention and Pan Janek and his measuring, but I did not dwell upon it for too long.

It began to snow four days before Christmas Eve. As soon as the first small flakes fell on the ground, Bella in my old coat and I in my new coat were out to play. The evening came so soon we were surprised when the streetlights went on. For awhile we watched the snow falling in the circles of light and then headed home. Bella was becoming a nuisance, repeatedly reminding me, "It's time to eat; it's time to eat."

I looked up, but our windows were dark. While we were climbing the staircase, I wondered where my parents were at this hour. We kept an extra key under the windowsill in the stairwell. I took it from its hiding place and opened the door to the apartment. Both Mama and Papa were sitting in the dark, so wrapped up in their conversation they didn't hear either the key in the lock or the door. Mama startled and jumped from her seat when she saw me standing in the doorway. I could tell she was scared.

"Why so dark?" I asked. She didn't answer but rushed past me to close and bolt the front door. She ushered us to the bathroom, closed the door, and then turned on the light.

Our bathroom had no window—only a vent above the door, which opened to a small hallway. Mama said to take off our clothes and shoes and shake off the snow into the tub, turn off the light before opening the door, and tiptoe directly to the back room. The back room (which we also occasionally called small room) was Grandma T's, Bella's, and mine. It was called the back room because it faced the courtyard of the building. Mama allowed us to turn on a small reading lamp, providing it was placed on the floor, and then she promised to bring us sandwiches and tea. Grandma T. was napping in her favorite corner by the window, clutching the rosary in her hands. I wanted to hear what was being said in the kitchen, so we left the door to the room opened and sat next to each other in the dark. Bella was afraid. She asked if she could hold my hand, and I let her.

The kitchen was lit by the glow of the streetlight coming through the window. Papa sat in the corner, by the table. Mama was moving about, fixing sandwiches. At intervals, hushed voices and scraps of conversation reached the threshold of the back room where we sat. After a while I was able to make out that Pan Janek was arrested last night. He was drunk when the men from the Secret Police came to get him. There was no telling whose names he gave them or what stories he fed them in drunken terror. His wife intercepted my father somewhere on his way back from work in order to warn him.

Father suspected that Pan Janek was a part of a scheme to smuggle much bigger things than American cigarettes and children's sheepskin coats. Mama said, "It smells like economic sabotage or selling state secrets." Then I heard that Father was planning to leave town for a couple of days to stay at Uncle Bert's, Bella's father. The day before Christmas Eve, Papa was to come back and get us, and we were to have Christmas at Bella's house. Upon hearing this Bella became very excited, but I was sorry we were not going to have our own Christmas tree this year.

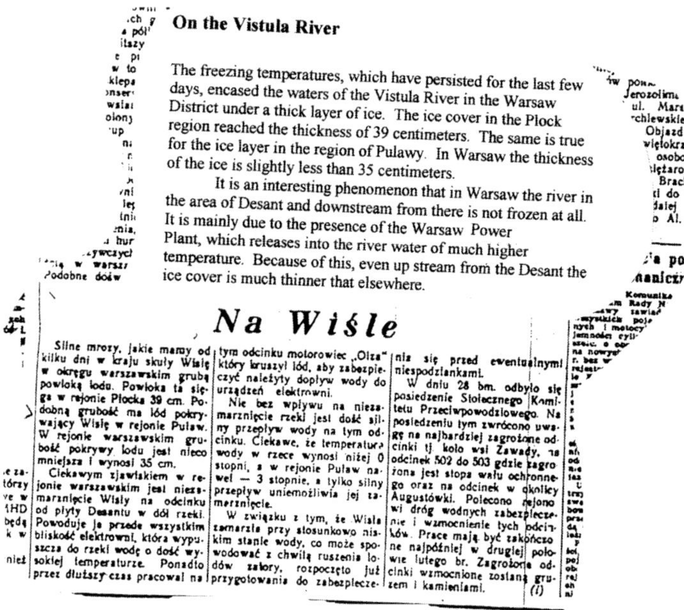

On the Vistula River

The freezing temperatures, which have persisted for the last few days, encased the waters of the Vistula River in the Warsaw District under a thick layer of ice. The ice cover in the Plock region reached the thickness of 39 centimeters. The same is true for the ice layer in the region of Pulawy. In Warsaw the thickness of the ice is slightly less than 35 centimeters.

It is an interesting phenomenon that in Warsaw the river in the area of Desant and downstream from there is not frozen at all. It is mainly due to the presence of the Warsaw Power Plant, which releases into the river water of much higher temperature. Because of this, even up stream from the Desant the ice cover is much thinner that elsewhere.

The day Papa was to come home and get us, Mama was packing clothes and holiday provisions. She said Bella and I were in the way, so I dragged out from the back of the closet my wooden sled, and we planned a trip all the way to the dike. It was the only decent hill in the neighborhood, and everyone who owned a sled was going to be there that morning. We climbed to the top of the dike, and the white river unfolded before us. The untouched, empty expanse of ice was beautiful beyond words and terribly tempting.

Bella and I made a few runs on our sled from the top of the dike. In spite of the fact that it was fun and that we had plenty of company, my heart wasn't in it. It was on the river. I imagined riding the ice like a snow queen, whipping thousands of white bees into a dust cloud of shimmering light. When we reached the top of the dike again, I told Bella to sit on the sled, and I pulled it down the other side and onto the ice. The sled glided easily, as if by itself. I ran as fast as I could, pulling Bella behind me. It was getting hot, so I unbuttoned my green coat and let it fly in the wind as I ran and ran. On the open face of the ice, it was much windier than behind the dike. The wind had cold fingers, and I felt its touch through my sweater and undershirt. After awhile we traded places. The sled on the ice was so light that Bella easily pulled the weight much larger than herself. Here and now I was really flying. We stopped where I thought was the middle of the river. Some kids on the dike were waving and yelling something to us, but their voices were muffled by the wind and the distance. We were alone in an endless white field, and our tracks in the thin layer of snow, which covered the ice, were already being blown over.

"It's so great," I said to Bella "I think I'm going to cry!"

"But you won't," she said, looking worriedly into my face. I knew she didn't want me to cry. We had this silent agreement between us that said that I was not the one who cried. So I didn't. The bridge from which I first saw this winter river was quite close now. I could see trams, buses, and cars go by, but they seemed to be moving in silence. The sounds of traffic were dispersed by the wind before reaching the surface of the ice. It was beautiful here. It was quiet. Even the wind talked only in whispers.

Tram number nine stopped in the middle of the bridge, and a man in the black coat, much like Papa's, got out. He ran to the railing and started waving his arms in a very agitated manner. He must have been yelling something too, but the sound never reached us. We just started on a new game of making elaborate patterns with our feet and sled in the snow upon the ice.

In the course of the game, we covered about two thirds of the distance across the river toward the opposite bank. When I looked up, I saw the man in the black coat running over the ice in our direction. I watched him for some time and became convinced that it was, indeed, my father, and that he must have recognized my green coat from the bridge. Just then, I realized that he might also be a bit upset about our excursion and decided to get ashore as quickly as I could. Since the shortest way to the bank was now ahead of us, I told Bella to get on the sled and broke into a sprint in its direction. Through the wind and the flapping of my coat tails, I could now hear Father yelling and panting quite clearly. The bank of the river was only a few yards away, but it was very steep and iced over. It took me some time to pull the sled, with Bella on it, just a bit up the slope. I looked up at the bridge. People had gathered along the railing. They were waving and clapping their hands.

Father was closing upon us, and I could see he was raging mad. I was trying in my mind to run through my options before he reached the bank when I heard a low thud and a hissing noise. Father stood frozen in the middle of the intricate spider web of cracks, which surrounded him and gathered at his feet. His face was gray, and he seemed to have shrunk. We all waited in silence for the hissing sound, as if for a spider to spring upon its helpless victim. He was just four yards from the bank, but the river on this side was deep and swift and dangerous. Minutes passed, and we waited. Father spoke in a low but very calm voice.

"Undo the string on the sled and run it through the sleeves of your coat then tie it back to the sled." he said.

By the time I was finished, two men made their way down from the top of the bridge. They pushed the sled back onto the ice and held on to the tails of my coat. The sled glided easily and stopped almost at Papa's feet. He knelt to grab a hold of it, and the ice began to hiss again. Amidst the hissing and cracking, the men pulled him to the edge of the ice and then onto the bank. He was violently shaking. They helped him sit down on a large boulder, and one of them lit and handed him a cigarette. He inhaled deeply and started to cough. Tears ran down his cheeks, and I didn't know if it was from the cold or from coughing that he was crying. One of the men asked him if he was all right, and he said he was. Then the two men climbed up the bank and headed toward the spiral staircase, which led to the top of the bridge. For some time, Father continued smoking and gazing on the ground between his feet. Bella and I sat quietly on a boulder few steps up the hill. Both times, now and when he was trapped in the middle of the icy spider web, he struck me as being a very small man. I understood that his life was like walking on ice that could start cracking and hissing at any time. He was trapped like a small fly in a web of circumstances. And although he was a man of quick decisions, simple solutions, and fierce energy, he was doomed because he was born in this city and by this river, which at that time was a wrong place to be born. Because of who he was, he could not be saved from continually walking on the ice, and all I could do was love him no matter what happened next. Finally he rose heavily and threw his cigarette butt into the snow. He looked very tired.

"Go on; get your coat," he said. "We're going home."